LEGACY OF LOVE

Bookseller Kay Deacon learns that she has been left part of the late Tobias Garner's collection of antique books on condition she brings his records up to date. So when Tobias's nephew Marshall Garner accuses her of cultivating the old man's affections, Kay resolves to carry out Tobias's wishes and prove that she is not a gold digger. But when she begins to find herself entangled in a web of deceit, her own life is in danger . . .

DOROTHY TAYLOR

LEGACY OF LOVE

Complete and Unabridged

LINFORD
Leicester

First published in Great Britain in 2008

First Linford Edition
published 2009

British Library CIP Data

Taylor, Dorothy.
    Legacy of love
    1. Love stories.
    2. Large type books.
    I. Title
    823.9′2–dc22 [F]

    ISBN 978–1–84782–645–9

Published by
F. A. Thorpe (Publishing)
Anstey, Leicestershire

Set by Words & Graphics Ltd.
Anstey, Leicestershire
Printed and bound in Great Britain by
T. J. International Ltd., Padstow, Cornwall

This book is printed on acid-free paper

1

Eager to be out of the bitter April wind, Kay Deacon hurried into the premises of Hinchcliffe, Mandale and Burton, the local firm of solicitors situated directly across the cobbled square from her bookshop.

Like many of the businesses in the old Derbyshire town centre, it had long been converted from a domestic residence into a commercial one.

A cheerful greeting from the smartly-dressed brunette Kay judged to be in her forties, was as warm and welcome as the central heating and went some way in calming her growing feelings of apprehension.

'Miss Deacon?'

'Yes.' Kay returned her smile. 'I received a letter from a Mr Adams last week asking me to call today.' She lifted the flap of her roomy tan leather shoulder-bag ready to take out the solicitor's letter.

'Regarding the will of the late Tobias Henry Garner.'

'That's right.'

'I'm Jane Brookes, Mr Adam's secretary. D'you happen to have the letter with you?' She got up and came out from behind her desk.

'Yes, I have.' Digging deep, Kay handed it over.

After a brief glance at the contents, Mrs Brookes gave it back. 'That's fine. I'll just pop upstairs and let Mr Adams know you're here. The family members arrived a short time ago. Please take a seat.'

Alone, Kay crossed her feet under the chair and looked around the neatly laid out office for some distraction.

Just as she checked her watch the door opened again.

'If you'd like to come up now,' Jane Brookes smiled.

'Yes, of course.' The invitation flipped Kay's stomach over. She got up unsure of what to expect.

Upstairs on the first floor she was ushered into a large room at the front of the building and immediately felt at home amongst the heavy old fashioned furniture cramping it.

While Kay's attention was immediately taken by the silver-haired solicitor rising to his feet, she was also aware of the three other people in the room.

'Miss Deacon, Mr Adams' Jane Brookes announced.

'Thank you, Mrs Brooks. Miss Deacon, please do come and join us.' He came out from behind his large dark desk and offered his hand. 'Samuel Adams, senior partner.'

'Mr Adams.' She responded with a smile, at the same time aware of a chill in the air which had nothing to do with the persistent wind rattling the windows but everything to do with the stony-faced man standing in profile at them.

Hands in the trouser pockets of his black formal suit, his manner suggested he was deeply absorbed in the comings and goings of the town square.

In the centre of the room a pretty young girl also dressed in black, sat slightly hunched in one of a pair of green leather armchairs in front of the cast-iron fireplace.

'And thank you for coming so promptly.' Samuel Adams caught her attention again. 'Now would you care for a cup of tea?'

Kay declined with a smile. 'No thank you, Mr Adams.'

'In that case,' he glanced across the room towards the window, 'may I introduce Mr Marshall Garner, the late Mr Garner's nephew.'

Gaining no response other than a dark look, he cleared his throat and with his composure slightly ruffled, turned to complete the introductions. 'His niece, Miss Lucinda Garner and nephew, Mr Niall Stevens.'

Lucinda acknowledged Kay with a small smile as Niall stepped forward and offered his hand. 'Nice to meet you,' he said. Immediately her spirits lifted. His deep tones were pleasant and Kay liked him straight away.

'Please take a seat, Miss Deacon.' Marshall Garner's command rang out before she had time to return Niall's greeting.

Turning her head in some surprise, his silver grey eyes were now scrutinising her own warm gaze with an animosity she found disturbing.

Marshall Garner gestured impatiently towards another empty armchair close to where he was standing. 'This chair is free. I'm sure you're just as eager as I am to get this over with.'

'The one here will be fine,' she rallied quickly, flashing him a steely look.

'Ah, yes. To the matter in hand.' Clearly flustered, Samuel Adams took his seat again. 'As I mentioned before, the suddenness of your uncle's death came as a great shock to the community. I realise it's of little consolation, but he did have the foresight to ensure his affairs were always kept up to date. Apart from some recent changes it is all very straightforward.'

As the solicitor paused to open an embossed folder, Kay felt the atmosphere drop several more degrees.

'Apart from a number of small gifts to several life-long friends and colleagues and some charitable donations,' the solicitor continued, 'I can confirm the main beneficiaries are yourself, Mr Garner, Miss Lucinda Amelia Garner, Mrs Helen Constance Stevens, her son, Niall Arthur Stevens, and Miss Kay Deacon, the owner of Deacon's Antiquarian Books. The details are as follows . . .'

Primed the family members would probably be mentioned first, Kay withdrew her attention to what was being said.

'And finally, as one I know who shares my love of the written word . . .'

Instinctively Kay picked up on what was being said and braced herself as Samuel Adams gave her a glance of encouragement. ' . . . and whom I feel sure will take good care of what became my lifelong work, I hereby bequeath to Miss Kay Deacon the following.'

'The bequest is part of Mr Garner's private library,' he went on to explain. 'And comprises a fairly lengthy list. Rather than read it out, I have had a copy printed for you.' He handed her a large envelope.

In something of a daze, Kay took it. Old Tobias had left her part of his collection?

Marshall Garner's attitude should thaw now he realised she hadn't been left the family jewels, she considered wryly.

She risked another glance in his direction, disconcerted to have it snatched and held with such spellbinding effect.

'Uncle Toby's books!' Lucinda's exclamation killed the moment.

Kay turned her attention to the young girl. Niall, she noticed, seemed temporarily lost in thought.

Marshall Garner made no comment.

'Hope you have room for them,' Niall

said, smiling again. 'Uncle Toby had rather a lot.'

'I'm sure I'll find space somewhere in my flat,' she answered. 'If not,' she paused, an idea taking shape. She turned back to the solicitor. 'Mr Adams, would there by any objection to my donating some to the town Library's reference section in Mr Garner's memory? I'm sure they'd be appreciated.'

'That shouldn't be a problem,' the solicitor responded. 'Naturally under the terms of the will, the family has first refusal. But for the moment that is not a matter of urgency.'

Kay frowned. 'It's not?'

'There is a condition to the bequest which may have some bearing on whether you decide to accept it or not.'

For a moment Kay was thrown. From the corner of her eye she sensed renewed interest in Marshall and Niall's demeanour, while Lucinda hunched closer to the fire and began to study her nails.

'There is an added proviso,' Samuel continued. 'Before you have authority to remove the books, the catalogues pertaining to the collection must be brought up to date by yourself in situ at Westwood, the family home.'

Kay frowned, totally bemused.

'I'm sure in your business capacity you were well aware Mr Garner took a great interest in antiquarian books. Records of his acquisitions, I'm led to believe, were kept scrupulously up to date until his health began to fail. With the knowledge of this particular idiosyncrasy his request does not appear too unusual.'

'If you are prepared to accept this condition and complete the necessary work — ' he broke off, looking across the tops of his glasses at Marshall, 'for which Mr Garner, I must add, no time limit has been attached.'

With no reaction from him other than a brief nod, Samuel Adams turned to Kay. 'The stipulated books will be yours to do with as you wish. If you have no desire, or are unable to fulfil the requirement, the collection will automatically revert back to the family.'

'I understand,' Kay responded, still puzzling over Tobias's strange request.

Business concluded, Samuel Adams gathered the papers into one neat pile before replacing them in the folder.

While Kay continued to wonder what the required cataloguing would involved, Marshall's curt, 'Well, I trust you are not too disappointed, Miss Deacon,' did not register.

She frowned across at him. 'I'm sorry?'

'Having cultivated my uncle's affections maybe you were expecting something more than books.'

Beyond the shock of Marshall's accusation, Kay registered Lucinda's look of confusion.

By contrast, Niall appeared embarrassed. She sensed he was about to say something but instead steepled his fingers against his chin and stared at the carpet.

She pulled herself together and got to her feet. 'I shan't dignify your comments with a response, Mr Garner,' she said crisply. 'Other than they are an insult to your uncle's memory.'

She took some comfort in the dark stain colouring the taut line of his cheekbones before she turned back to the solicitor. 'If there's nothing more, Mr Adams, I must get back to work.'

'Of course, my dear, of course.' Within a charged atmosphere, Samuel Adams hastened to his feet; his eagerness to show her out apparent.

As he watched Kay go, Marshall still couldn't believe this young woman with the most liquid brown eyes he'd ever seen, was Toby's Kay Deacon.

He turned back to the window. Well yes, on second thoughts, having met her he could see exactly why his uncle had praised her almost to the point of being besotted. She would turn any man's head — even a confirmed bachelor in his sixties.

Behind his back his knuckles whitened as a fresh wave of anger overcame his grief. She had obviously been playing him along. Who knows what the outcome might have been if Toby hadn't had his heart attack.

Remorse then dissipated his anger. If only he'd not taken it upon his own shoulders to oversee the New Zealand contract and concentrated his efforts on working more in the UK.

If he'd moved back to England, taken time to check out what that lovable old bookworm had been telling him about his 'delightful friend in the town's bookshop' things might have been a whole lot different.

'Penny for them, Marshall?'

Marshall stiffened. From across the room the sound of Niall's voice obliterated his heated imaginings in one sober instant.

He turned to him and frowned. 'Believe me,' he gritted, 'they're not worth even that.'

'Could you give me a few days to

think this over?' Kay asked once they'd reached the bottom of the staircase.

'Naturally, my dear,' Samuel Adams enthused while still looking troubled. He nodded towards his secretary's office. 'Just give Mrs Brookes a call once you've decided what you want to do and we'll take it from there.' He lowered his voice. 'Please accept my apologies on Mr Garner's behalf. It's been a very difficult time. He's utterly — '

Objectionable. Kay expressed a silent opinion.

'Honestly, Mr Adams, there's no need,' she interrupted, raising her hand to brush aside what she suspected to be an apology on behalf of the last person on earth she felt deserved one. 'I appreciate your patience and I will get back to you soon.'

2

Kay flung open the shop door with more force than she'd intended startling her close friend and assistant manager, Rachel Thornton.

'Good grief, Kay.' Wide-eyed, Rachel looked up from behind the counter. 'Where's the fire?' Then she noticed Kay's tense expression. 'Something's wrong,' she frowned. 'I'll put the kettle on while the shop's empty.'

Crossing the shop floor she followed Rachel into the smallest of the two back rooms used as a kitchen. It had just enough space for them to put their feet up when the opportunity arose. The other room doubled as Kay's office and stock room.

She shrugged off her coat and draped it over the back of a chair then smoothed down her soft blue sweater and straight navy skirt. 'Although right

14

now I feel like going upstairs for something stronger.'

'Oh, yes?' Rachel's brow rose. 'That doesn't sound like you.'

'Well, as it's just been implied by Mr Garner's nephew that I'm some kind of gold digger, I'm having a bit of an identity crisis at the moment.'

Rachel spun round sending her dark curls bobbing. 'He did what?'

Kay frowned. 'What were his words now? Ah yes. Something about cultivating his uncle's affections.'

Rachel's blue eyes widened. 'Old Mr Garner? Is he crazy or something?'

'Well he certainly appeared mad at my being a beneficiary in the will.'

'The poor old thing,' Rachel mused, teapot in hand. 'If Mr Garner had any idea of what you've been accused of he'd be mortified.'

Feeling the after-effects of such an upsetting experience, Kay sank on to a low cushioned chair, thankful that for once the shop wasn't busy.

She closed her eyes briefly picturing

again Marshall's stern features. From her chats with Tobias, he more than lived up to the mental image she'd painted. Late twenties, tall, and despite bearing a profile carved out of granite, it pained her to admit he was good looking.

And most of all, he carried an air of being in authority; proved by his success as an expert in structural engineering, as Tobias had recounted on more than one occasion.

But at the expense of someone supposedly close to him, she decided. For when she'd asked if the old man saw much of him, she'd not missed a longing in his eyes as he'd said Marshall was far too busy travelling the world to spend much time at home.

'Here you are.' Rachel's voice had Kay opening her eyes again.

'That didn't take long.' She took the mug Rachel was offering. 'Thanks,' she sighed. 'I'm more than ready for this.'

'So,' Rachel leaned back against the kitchen unit from where she had a view of the stop's front door, 'tell me what happened?'

Kay gave her a wry look. 'You're not going to believe this,' she began.

A short while later Rachel said, 'You're right, I can't. The man's a monster. Forget about him,' Rachel encouraged. 'So Mr Garner left you part of his collection. I'm not that surprised. You two got on so well. It's strange he wants you to see his cataloguing is up to date, though. Wonder why?'

'I've been thinking the same,' Kay sighed. 'Still, that's how things stand. I'll have to arrange with Mr Adams to go round to Westwood some time soon and get an idea of what needs to be done.'

Later, an elderly couple walked into the shop. After browsing the shelves for a while, they sought Kay's advice.

'We're looking for something for our grandson,' the man began.

'Yes, he's twelve next week,' his wife explained proudly. 'Lives, eats and breathes astronomy.'

'But we're not quite sure of what's best,' her husband picked up.

Amused by the couple's interaction, Kay said, 'If you'd like to follow me. We have a section over here.'

She was stretching up to take down a number of books for the couple to mull over when the doorbell announced another arrival.

'Take a look through these,' she suggested, handing the books over. 'And if you need any more help, don't hesitate to ask.'

As she made her way back to the counter, she glanced across the shop to see who else had come in. But the dark-haired man in a navy blue overcoat, had his back to her as he browsed the shelves and was partly obscured by the tall, free-standing unit which took up most of the central space.

From behind a display unit, Marshall couldn't help but overhear Kay Deacon's conversation with her customers.

He'd seen her the moment he'd walked into the shop. Honed in on her with a speed and accuracy that had him wondering about his motives.

He continued to eavesdrop, glimpsed the ease in which she related to her elderly customers; becoming aware of her patience and good humour as she answered their questions.

Maybe he'd got it wrong. Maybe she really was the person Toby had made her out to be. No, he wasn't convinced. Still, with what he had planned he would soon confirm his suspicions. He frowned. Curiously he was not now quite so eager to prove the point.

As the satisfied couple moved away from the counter, Kay's smile faded at the sight of Marshal Garner turning round from one of the display stands as the couple walked past him.

She braced herself as he made his way towards the counter, his silver-grey eyes glittering and his expression just as grim as she remembered.

Just in time she mastered the beginnings of a shiver which threatened to race down her spine.

'Miss Deacon.'

He appeared at pains to be civil while, she suspected, not meaning a bit of it.

'Mr Garner,' she acknowledged coolly.

'So you are the owner of an antiquarian book shop?'

She challenged him with a direct gaze. 'You find something improbable about that?'

His eyes narrowed. 'No,' he said. 'Not at all.' Yet his assessing look belied his words.

Her gaze didn't falter. 'It's a family business,' she said crisply. 'My parents retired last year and moved to Spain. I took over the running of it then.'

'And that's how you met my uncle?'

She continued to match his cold regard. 'Your uncle was a well-known figure around town, Mr Garner. Like most local people I was on nodding terms with him. Once I began to work full time for my father, I got to know him better.'

'Know him better.' His words were laced with cynicism.

She frowned at the underlying assumption. But before she could challenge him he added, 'So you come from around here?'

'I was born and raised here,' she replied curtly. She was fast losing patience with this interrogation. 'What is this . . . the third degree?'

A frown scored his brow. 'Not at all. Just interesting to finally put a face to a name. Although to be honest — '

To her growing resentment he eyed her up and down again, 'As a, er . . . friend of Toby's I was expecting tweeds, thick stockings and sensible shoes.'

There he went again. The emphasis on *friend*.

'Oh really?' she responded through gritted teeth. She recalled Tobias's praise of the man standing in front of her. 'Don't you find expectations sometimes have a habit of not being fulfilled? I found that was the case today. Still I'm sure your uncle wouldn't have deliberately misled you, Mr Garner.'

He frowned. 'That may well be. But surely there can be no greater puzzle than a woman taking a keen interest in a man, at a guess I'd say forty years her senior?' His mouth curved cynically as his silver eyes bore into hers. 'Then again is it? If her own interests are to be served, maybe it's not so surprising at all.'

Kay felt sick to her stomach. This was turning nasty.

She gave him a poisonous look. 'Just what are you implying?'

Not the least bit perturbed, he countered this question with a derisory expression that would have a lesser woman bursting into tears and dashing from the room. 'D'you really want me to spell it out?'

Kay felt the colour drain from her face. It was time she set the record straight. Focusing firmly on his accusing eyes, she said, 'Everything I had to do with your late uncle was strictly on a professional basis. I'm not the only person in town who thought a lot of him. We are all going to miss him very much. Now have you come here solely to continue my character assassination or are you looking to purchase a book?'

'Maybe some other time. What I'm here for now won't take long.'

She tried not to allow his gaze to bother her and made a point of looking at the shop clock.

'Good. It's right on closing time.'

She walked out from behind the counter and strode over to the shop door. After turning the closed sign around, she locked the door.

The few moments respite from his superior attitude gave her added strength to combat his manner.

Without a word he reached inside his overcoat, drew out a folded piece of paper and offered it to her.

'This should compensate for what

you may have been expecting,' he said.

As his mouth returned to its familiar firm line, she took the paper from him and opened it. It was a cheque made out to her for a sum which took her breath away.

Eyes large with shock, she looked back up at him. 'I don't understand.'

'It's not that difficult surely,' he dismissed coldly. 'This will save you the trouble of carrying out Toby's last wishes. As soon as I have the time I'll see the books he's bequeathed to you are professionally valued. If it turns out they are worth more than I've estimated, I'll see you get the difference.'

'That's very considerate of you,' she said coolly, folding the cheque again.

Despite wanting to rail against the continual misjudgement, she met his gaze with cold regard. 'Is that it then. Or is there anything else before you go?'

While his expression remained inscrutable, she sensed behind it something other than the satisfaction of being proved right.

Disappointment?

Don't be ridiculous, she chided herself.

'I doubt it,' he told her curtly. 'Now that I can safely assume our business is at an end.'

'You can?'

His eyes narrowed. His expression became so fierce her nerve almost crumbled. 'Now look — '

'No. You look,' she cut in bitterly.

Before he could say another word she tore his cheque in half then in half again and thrust the pieces back at him.

Taken by surprise, Marshall reacted automatically and took them off her.

'Again you've got it wrong,' she flared back at him. 'If it takes forever, I'll carry out your uncle's wishes just to please and respect his memory. So you might as well get used to the idea.'

For a moment he seemed strangely at a loss. Then he rallied. 'In that case you will need the address. That's if you don't already have it.'

Kay bit back a stinging reply and said

instead, 'I have a phone number, that's all. Although I did know your uncle lived somewhere near West Throwley.'

Marshall reached into his coat pocket again and took out a pen. 'D'you have something I could write the address on?'

Without a word, she slid a notepad towards him then watched as he hurriedly wrote down the details.

'D'you have any idea when you can begin the work?'

'Not exactly. If it's convenient, I'd like to take a look at the collection first to gain some idea of what's involved.'

'Not a problem.' Was she imagining it or were his eyes a little less cold.

'When would you like to call out to the house?'

'The shop's closed Sundays. Is this weekend too short notice.?'

'Not at all.'

For some unfathomable reason she found she couldn't hold his gaze. She glanced at the pad again, making out she was re-checking what he'd written.

Why was it, she fretted, that every time she encountered him she felt she was floundering in a turbulent sea of emotion?

'Sunday it is.' He broke the silence. 'I'll expect you around, say, three o'clock, if that suits?'

Kay met his eyes again and nodded her agreement. 'Yes, that's fine.'

While he manoeuvred his broad physique around the units, she remembered she needed to unlock the shop door.

She followed after and found herself admiring his shoulders, the way his dark hair grew at the back.

'Goodnight, Miss Deacon.' Marshall paused for a moment outside on the pavement.

With leaden limbs she made her way upstairs to her flat.

3

In uplifting contrast to the start of the week, as the weekend grew nearer the weather turned sunny and golden, with cotton wool clouds barely moving in an unbelievable blue sky.

After a busy day in the shop, Kay gave silent thanks that the local supermarket stayed open until eight as she hurried across the square.

Kay pulled out a trolley from the line waiting to be used and made her way down the first aisle. Before long she had everything she'd gone in for.

As she joined the queue at one of the three checkouts, the same question she'd puzzled over for days returned. Why had Tobias included her as a beneficiary in his will?

The number of titles he'd bequeathed to her had come as a shock, albeit a pleasant one. Some she'd recognised.

Others held the exciting promise of something yet undiscovered.

'Ah, we meet again.'

The deep, cheerful tones coming from behind Kay's shoulder broke her chain of thought.

She turned her head and met a smile as warm as she remembered. Niall Stevens was just about to begin loading the belt with a few items of groceries and several bottles of wine.

'Mr Stevens.'

He raised a brow. 'Niall, please.'

'Niall,' she repeated, matching his smile.

'Better day than Monday.'

'In more ways than one,' Kay said with feeling.

'I take it you mean Marshall.'

Conscious of the people queuing either side, he lowered his voice. 'I can only apologise for my cousin. I'm well used to the way he goes about things. But it must come as a shock for those who don't know him.'

'You could say that.' Her mood

suddenly blighted, Kay was swift to agree. Then it was her turn at the till.

'D'you need a hand?' A few minutes later Niall came over to the customer packing space where Kay was filling a third carrier. 'Looks like you have a lot there.'

'More bulk than weight,' she commented. 'But a hand would be very welcome if you're sure I won't be taking you out of your way. My flat's above the bookshop.'

'Across the square! I can just about manage that,' he teased.

Kay smiled. She was beginning to enjoy his company.

Fully expecting they would walk the short distance, she was surprised when Niall led the way to a gleaming red sports car parked a little further up the road.

'You're going to drive?' she questioned as he took the carriers from her and began to load them into the boot.

'Why not,' he grinned. 'Jump in.'

Shaking her head, she got in and

settled back into the comfortable cream leather passenger seat.

His pride in the vehicle was obvious. 'I thought so too,' he enthused, 'when it came into the showroom I just had to have her. I'll take you for a spin some time. Can't do full justice around town.'

'The car park's round the back,' she pointed ahead to the access road as Niall drove up to the bookshop barely moments later.

'Come on in,' she invited after he insisted on carrying her bags up the turned stone staircase at the rear of the building. 'Kitchen's through here.'

Once inside the bright compact kitchen he placed the carriers on to one of the counters then looked around the cheerful yellow décor. 'Very nice,' he nodded appreciatively. 'D'you live here alone?'

'Yes. I took over the business when my parents retired.'

'Must be interesting work. If you're into books.'

'It is,' she smiled. 'Would you like a coffee?'

'I've a better idea,' he grinned. 'Save you the bother. How about we pop into the local hostelry instead?'

'The Weavers?'

'The very one,' Niall nodded.

Why not, Kay decided. 'Yes I'd love to,' she agreed. 'Just let me put the shopping away first.'

The lively atmosphere inside the Weaver's Rest greeted them the moment Niall held open the door for her and Kay slipped inside.

Behind and above their seats, knick-knacks from bygone ages covered the sill and higher shelving. Horse brasses pinned to the ancient beams supporting the whitewashed ceiling reflected the log fire's flickering flames.

'This is the one thing Dad misses,' Kay said after Niall sat down beside her. 'Get togethers with his old friends in the business. They meet up here about once a month.'

'You haven't kept up the tradition, then?'

'No,' she chuckled. 'Hardly my age

group. Although I do come in occasionally with friends. It has a great atmosphere.'

After taking an enthusiastic swallow from his pint of local ale, Niall agreed. 'I usually pop in when I'm up to see my mother.'

'She lives around here?'

'Never left the district. Family home is a ten minute drive away.'

'Oh, I see.' So Niall was local, too.

'I moved to Manchester with work years ago.' His expression grew a little sombre. 'Mother's housebound now; not so good on her feet.'

'Oh, I'm sorry.'

He shrugged. 'Aunt Vi, her sister-in-law, lives with her and they have a daily help. I make a point of coming across as often as I can. The time will come when she'll probably need residential care but,' he brightened again, 'for the moment things are manageable. So Kay, you're a bookseller and your parents have retired. Only child?'

She nodded.

'Like me. Stop me if I'm being nosey, but I'd love to know more.'

Maybe it was the wine combined with Niall's likeable personality, but it wasn't long before she'd given him a potted history of the Deacon family, going back to her great-grandfather.

Niall nodded. 'So Derbyshire born and bred with books in your blood?'

Kay laughed. 'Grandfather started the business so you could say it's something I've inherited. Books tend to occupy me most of the time. Particularly the rare ones. I must sound like an anorak.'

'Well you certainly don't look like one.' Niall eyed her appreciatively. 'No wonder you and Uncle Toby got on so well. He was crazy about books, too. So what about the collection. Are you really going to catalogue it?'

'I'm hoping to,' she said thoughtfully. 'I'll have to take a look at what needs to be done.'

'But you could be taking on a lot you know. I should imagine Marshall would be willing to come to some agreement; give you their value instead. He'd pay you what the books are worth. Save you a lot of bother.'

It was on the tip of her tongue to say he'd already done just that but she held back. Instead she shook her head. 'No. I owe it to your uncle to take a look, if nothing else.'

'Of course. Perhaps I shouldn't have said what I did. So when d'you plan on calling out to Westwood?'

'This Sunday.'

Niall looked surprised.

'I arranged it with your cousin the day the will was read.'

'Oh, I see.' He frowned. 'He doesn't let the grass grow under his feet.'

Probably wants to see the back of me as soon as possible, Kay reflected silently as she took another sip from her glass.

'Well, I've no idea what the rest of his plans are regarding his work,' Niall said. 'Keeps things close to his chest. Hopefully he'll be off on his travels again before much longer. A word of advice. Don't let him get to you. Lucy and I have both felt the lash of his tongue at times.'

'Oh?' His words intrigued but he didn't elaborate further.

Instead he said, 'Next time I'm up, perhaps we could see each other. Have dinner?'

'Yes I'd like that.'

'Great.' Niall slapped his knee. 'Could be a couple of weeks though; pressure of work and all that. But the first opportunity, I'll be up here like a shot.'

★ ★ ★

The following Sunday, Kay set off for West Throwley, a small village some thirty miles away and was soon driving through lush, hilly farmland crisscrossed with dry stone walls.

It was a deceptively sunny day; the sky deep blue, yet along the roadside's grassy banks, daffodils and wild primroses shivered in the chill wind.

The road climbed for a good part of her journey until she reached the summit. Then below her the buttery stonework of West Throwley village came into view, nestling in the folds of the surrounding hills.

As the tree-lined road brought her closer to her destination, the only blot on her horizon was a growing sense of apprehension to be meeting Marshall Garner again.

The sight of two tall gateposts gracing the entrance to a wide gravelled drive told her she'd arrived. Lofty wrought iron gates stood open.

Mentally crossing her fingers, she turned off the empty road and steered her car through.

At first, the sweeping drive, widely bordered with evergreen shrubs and carpeted with the bright blues, white and yellows of countless spring flowers, hid any sign of the house but moments later there was Westwood's lofty pale stone construction standing before her.

She pulled up to one side of the open

ridged porch protecting the studded front door.

She entered the porch and saw an old-fashioned bell-pull to one side of the door.

Taking a steadying breath she reached over and grasped it.

4

It came as some surprise when Marshall Garner answered the door. From the size of the house, Kay had been expecting a housekeeper to attend to that for him.

And how different he looked from the formally-suited businessman the first time they'd met. The casual cut of his navy-blue polo shirt and faded denims seemed to make him more human, more approachable.

All three shirt buttons were open at the neck and she could see the beginnings of dark silky chest hair against his tanned skin. The short sleeves exposed the same dark swirls accentuating the masculine strength of his forearms.

But his greeting held the formality she'd been expecting. 'Miss Deacon. Please come in.'

'Thank you.' Once inside, Kay looked around with interest at the square oak-panelled hall graced by an ornately-carved turned staircase which rose far above them. At the same time the chimes of a gleaming grandfather clock struck the hour.

'Prompt as ever,' Marshall said.

She shot him a glance, unsure how to judge his tone. However, the lines of his face now appeared a little more relaxed, so she took his comment as a compliment.

'My father's influence.' She gave him a half smile. 'He always says a successful business reflects an ordered mind.'

'Wise man.'

'I've realised it's the only way to keep on top of things.'

Then surprisingly, 'You must miss your parents.'

She met his gaze. 'Yes, I do. But as Dad got older he suffered badly with arthritis. Spain's dry climate is perfect for him.' This time her smile was lit with warmth. 'He's taken on a new lease of life since they emigrated; golf, swimming, any activity you can think of. Mum's thriving on it, too.'

A frown crossed Marshall's brow. 'That must be a great relief.'

'Well, yes. Yes, it is.' So much for thinking things were improving, she told herself, noting his changed expression.

'Would you like to go straight to the library,' he invited. 'Or would you prefer a hot drink before we begin? It's quite a long drive from town to here.'

A hot drink sounded really appealing and it must have shown on her face. Before she had chance to agree, Marshall said, 'Tea or coffee?'

'A coffee would be very welcome.'

He guided her around a central dark oval table into a corridor on the left.

Very much Tobias, Kay reflected noticing a collection of oil paintings, mainly of local landscapes, hung on both walls.

They continued past several closed

doors until they reached the door at the end.

'Help yourself to a chair while I see to the coffee,' Marshall said as he ushered Kay inside. 'Mrs Talbot has the day off. It's her niece's birthday.'

Kay wandered over the quarry-tiled floor and choose one of a pair of chintz-covered armchairs set near an old cast iron range.

Soon the aroma of freshly-ground coffee filled the air with its own special allure.

'Cream and sugar?' Marshall called over.

'Just as it comes, please, Mr Garner.'

'Please call me Marshall. No-one stands on ceremony at Westwood.'

She hid her surprise by this show of informality and said, 'In that case, you must call me Kay.'

Moments later he joined her.

'Thank you.' Kay took the mug he offered then waited until he sat down in the facing chair before taking a sip from it.

'The collection,' Marshall said, looking across at her. 'I'm curious to know how you're going to tackle it?'

'I have been giving it some thought,' she admitted. 'And I can't see any other way than checking each book against your uncle's records. I have to say he's been very generous to me.'

'It was Toby's nature.'

'I know what you mean but it was still unexpected. I'm very touched.'

For a moment she sensed Marshall was lost in his own thoughts. Then he focused on her again.

'What d'you say to forgetting our differences?'

This time she had no doubt her surprise was showing.

'Differences?' she exclaimed, regarding him steadily. 'It was hardly that. You were the one throwing insults. I was merely standing up for myself.'

'I made a bad mistake.' The remorse in his eyes was uplifting. 'Please accept my apologies.'

'Apology accepted,' she smiled and

felt the tension lifting from her shoulders.

His quiet appreciation enhanced an unexpected glow in her heart until she told herself she was being foolish to react to him in such a way.

'I didn't realise this was your home, too,' she said, wanting to get on top of things again. 'I had the impression your uncle lived alone.'

'He did until fifteen years ago. I was fourteen when my parents were killed in a traffic accident, Lucy was almost three. Drunk driver,' he added with contempt.

Kay frowned, shocked by what he'd said. 'I'm sorry. I didn't mean — '

'You're not to know,' he dismissed swiftly. 'Toby raised us after that and no-one could have made a better job of it.'

'That must have been a huge consolation,' she said gently, sensing he was happy to continue.

Marshall nodded. 'As I said, he was the perfect substitute. He was Father's elder brother. Aunt Helen, Niall's mother, his younger sister. She's never enjoyed good health. Looking after another two children would have been too much for her.'

'Despite being a bachelor and an academic, Tobias had that special gift of being able to see the world from a child's point of view. Lucy adored him; she could wrap him round her little finger. Yes,' he sighed, 'he was a very special man.'

And then his expression revealed the sense of loss he was feeling and Kay began to understand Samuel Adam's attempts to explain the reason for Marshall's attitude at the reading of the will. He had been lashing out at the world and she had been the unfortunate focus of that attention.

'Can I smell coffee?' A voice from the doorway broke a momentary silence.

As Marshall turned his head, Kay looked over to see Lucinda coming into the room. The long strap of a roomy tasselled bag crossed a cerise woollen jacket beneath which figure-hugging blue and green vest tops and a long heavy green skirt, accentuated her slender finger.

'Hi, Marshall. Miss Deacon,' she acknowledged brightly. 'Heard you were coming today. Had your guided tour of the library yet?'

'I'll show Kay around after we've finished our coffee,' Marshall answered for her.

'Kay. Oh, right.' Lucinda shot Kay a grin. 'Everyone calls me Lucy, Kay, so you must do the same.'

'Hello again, Lucy,' Kay responded with a smile.

'Don't envy you going through Uncle Toby's old books. There's absolutely thousands of them.' Lucy continued to chat.

After hanging her bag on the back of a chair she sat down and turned to her brother. 'Marshall, can't Kay just have her books?'

'Your uncle wanted me to complete his records,' Kay reminded her. 'I couldn't take his bequest without doing so.'

'Kay's right, Lucy,' Marshall added. 'The least we can all do is respect Toby's wishes.'

'I get your point,' Lucy said, tossing back her long blonde hair. 'But how am I going to manage when I start uni and can't touch my trust fund until I'm twenty-one?'

'Lucy!' Marshall's expression immediately hardened.

Kay shifted uncomfortably in her chair.

'But it's the truth,' Lucy complained.

'And we've discussed this before,' Marshall warned. 'It will all be taken care of. The matter's closed.'

Lucy got to her feet. 'I'm going to my room. Oh, and I shan't be in for dinner,' she added, 'I'm seeing Darren tonight.'

Kay sensed Marshall stiffen. 'You know my feelings about him,' he retorted. 'He's a waster.'

As Lucy shot her brother a dark look,

Kay detected a shadow of misery behind the defiance in the young girl's eyes.

'That's a horrible thing to say,' Lucy pouted. 'He just hasn't found the right career yet.'

'So you say,' Marshall retorted. 'We'll discuss this some other time.'

As the kitchen door was closed with more force than was necessary, Marshall gave Kay a wry look. 'Sorry about that,' he sighed.

'Don't worry about it,' she said with some sympathy. 'Seventeen can be a difficult age and it's obvious Lucy's still upset over the death of your uncle.'

Marshall sighed. 'Yes, she has taken it rather badly. As for this boyfriend of hers.' He made a sound of contempt. 'I just hope once she begins her university course, the excitement of taking her first steps into adulthood will make her see him in a different light.'

'I'm sure it will,' Kay confirmed, remembering the good times with the whole new circle of friends she'd made when she'd taken her degree.

'What is she hoping to study?' she asked.

'Fashion Design.'

'I should have guessed,' Kay smiled. 'Her style of dress is that bit different. She has a certain flair.'

'Yes. She's very good. And that's not just family pride,' Marshall was quick to add. 'I've been assured if she keeps up her standard of course work, she'll be accepted wherever she applies.'

A frown returned. 'Trouble is, this boyfriend. He's not the type I imagined her falling for.' He shook his head. 'I have to play things very carefully. Lucy will be eighteen in September and free to do what she likes. I'm concerned she might do something stupid.' He sighed heavily. 'It's a worry.'

Kay attempted reassurance. 'I thought I knew it all when I was seventeen. Don't worry, it will pass.'

A flash of hope lit Marshall's eyes. 'I wonder — no, it's too much to ask.'

Puzzled Kay asked. 'What is?'

'I don't suppose you could have a chat to her while you're here; only if the opportunity arose, of course,' he hastened. 'She's barely had an older woman to confide in, if at all. I know you're not that much older, but — '

'I'm twenty-seven,' she told him and then her brown eyes teased. 'I think a ten year gap is wide enough. If you think it will help, I'll see what I can do.'

It was pleasing to see the tension of his jaw line ease into a smile. He should do that more often, she decided. It suits him.

Then the distant sound of a chiming clock reminded her why she was there.

'I think I should take a look at the collection now, don't you?'

In comfortable silence, they re-crossed the hall and entered the corridor directly opposite. It was a mirrored reflection of the other. Again more oils hung between a run of several closed doors.

At the end Kay noticed a pale wedge of light illuminating the dark olive runner.

Sensing this was the library, she felt a rush of excitement.

She found herself holding her breath as Marshall opened the door and ushered her inside.

'Oh!' was all she could say as the contents of the room appeared before her. Wide-eyed Kay gazed around the large rectangular room which held a calming air of peace and harmony.

She stepped on to the first of two beautiful Persian rugs overlaying the light oak floorboards, their muted tones picked out by a pair of rich burgundy curtains hanging either side of the french doors accessing the terrace, then paused by a mahogany worktable and continued to look around.

From floor to ceiling, two glass-fronted bookcases lined the walls either side of the door, but it was the long interior wall which mesmerised her more than anything else.

Again behind glass, from floor to ceiling volumes of all shapes and sizes filled every available shelf space.

There were acres and acres of books.

'I never imagined . . . ' She glanced up at Marshall.

He looked amused. Hoping fervently the majority had been catalogued, Kay walked with him over to the centre wall. If not, she worried, she could be here for weeks.

After reading numerous titles, she turned to him with a look of concern. 'This could turn out to be a major undertaking.'

Marshall's grey eyes swept the surrounding shelves. 'Yes, there are rather a lot,' he agreed thoughtfully. He quirked a dark brow. 'Second thoughts?'

Regret in his tone was a surprise. She shook her head. 'No, not at all. I was thinking more of how long it might take. I could be here for quite some time.'

His features lightened again. 'As far as I'm concerned, it's not a problem. You can come and go as you please. Stay as a house guest if you prefer while you're breaking the back of it. Mrs Talbot will see to your needs and Lucy will be around, of course. Although saying that,' he grimaced, 'she'll probably be a distraction.'

Kay smiled. 'A pleasant one, all the same.'

'If you say so,' he joked and Kay could tell he was pleased by her comment.

'It's likely I'll be away on business fairly often during the coming weeks,' Marshall said. 'In fact,' he paused briefly, 'if you could stay it would be an enormous help.'

Despite the friction she'd just witnessed between brother and sister, there was something appealing about Lucy; something she'd tuned into the other day at the solicitor's. 'But there is the shop to consider. I'll need to arrange cover if I stay.'

Marshall grimaced. 'Sorry. I'm asking too much.'

'No, no. It's not that,' Kay was quick to contradict. 'Rachel, my manager, will be quite happy to take over.'

'Thank you,' Marshall brightened. 'That would be perfect.'

'I'll get back to you in the morning to confirm,' she smiled. 'Now if I could just see your uncle's records, I'll have some idea of how up-to-date they are.'

'They're on the worktable. Let's take a look.'

Amongst several stacks of books, four large leather-bound ledgers stood out easily against the rest. On closer inspection, Kay realised the entwined design stamped in gold leaf on the front cover revealed the initials *THG*.

'Help yourself,' Marshall invited, pulling out a chair for her before bringing one around from the side for himself. 'As far as I know, they were kept up-to-date until Toby's health began to fail. Problem is, how many more books he'd acquired since then.' He shrugged, 'I've no idea.'

With Marshall sitting alongside her, she opened the first ledger and guessed by the date at the top of the page it would turn out to be the most recent of the four.

Neat entries of copperplate writing illuminated the pages with all the information she needed; titles, dates of purchase, values. Tucked inside the last page of entries were numerous scraps of paper with various notes and titles written on them.

'The notes could refer to the last lot of purchases.' Marshall said what Kay had been thinking. 'Looks like you'll have to check those with the shelves as well as the ledgers.'

'It's the only way,' she agreed, picking up another and opening it to find more of Tobias's notes. 'One good thing,' she was happy to tell him. 'Your uncle was pretty specific in categorising his purchases. If the shelving system matches them, it should make the work a lot easier.'

Marshall looked relieved. 'Let's hope that's the case.'

With Marshall's assistance, she was pleased to find the ledgers fitted snugly into her shoulder bag. Once secured, she covered the books with the protective leather flap.

'D'you mind if I just take a quick look at the ones by the door before I go?'

'Take all the time you need,' he encouraged. 'The keys are in the locks, so feel free to examine anything on the shelves.'

While Kay crossed the room, Marshall picked up a book off the table and settled down to wait on a Chesterfield sofa upholstered in the same burgundy velvet as the drapes.

She scanned the titles. Happy to see Tobias had categorised his books into subject order, she envisaged a routine of how to go about the work.

She also noticed the same patterned *THG*, written lightly in pencil on the inside of the back cover of each book she'd picked out at random.

After what felt like a matter of minutes, she checked her watch and was surprised to see she'd been at

Westwood for over two hours.

Marshall got to his feet as she rejoined him.

'It's time I was leaving,' she said.

'Sure you've seen enough?'

'For today, yes,' she smiled. 'It's an amazing collection. I'm looking forward to working on it.'

He appeared pleased by her comment. 'That should make things easier for you.'

Marshall saw her to her car. 'You'll let me know whether you'd like to stay or not?' he asked as she was just about to get in.

She paused briefly, battling once more to keep control of her hair as the wind snatched at it again. 'I'll ring as soon as I can.'

Marshall nodded. 'I'll be here. I'll look forward to your call.'

5

'Thought I'd find you in here.' Startled by the interruption Kay looked up from the entries she'd been going over a second time to see Niall coming into the library.

'Niall?' she frowned. 'I wasn't expecting to see you so soon.'

'Nice surprise, yeah?' he grinned as he walked over to where she was sitting at the worktable. 'So how's it going?'

He put his hand on the back of her chair and peered over her shoulder at the open pages of the ledger.

'Er, it's all been fine up to now,' she answered twisting round in the chair. 'But how did — '

'I get in?' He moved away and flopped down on to the sofa.

Kay's eyes widened a little as he raised his feet on to the low table in front of him then, leaning back, crossed one over the other.

'Well, yes,' she said. 'Mrs Talbot is down in the village doing some shopping. And I didn't hear the bell.'

It was beginning to irritate the way he was going about making himself at home with little regard for the beautiful sofa table. He folded his arms and glanced her way again. 'Had my own key for years. Used to keep a quiet eye on old Toby for Marshall when I was up. He's worked abroad for years now and with Lucy away at boarding school until she was sixteen, Toby was on his own most of the time. Apart from the Talbots, of course.'

'They're a nice couple,' Kay said. And very capable, she reflected. Nesta Talbot had the energy of someone half her age and her husband, Jack, who saw to the grounds and took care of small maintenance work, was a muscular giant of a man.

With the Talbots around, she couldn't imagine Marshall having any concerns about his uncle's welfare. But then again, who was she to know?

'Looks like you've got your work cut out,' Niall interrupted Kay's puzzlings.

Kay shrugged. 'I'm used to it. Remember, it's what I do for a living. The ones either side of the door tally perfectly with Tobias's ledgers. But,' she sighed, 'I've just started on the main shelving and hit a snag.'

'Oh,' Niall frowned. 'In what way?'

Kay played down the problem. 'I'm sure there's a perfectly good reason, but some of the books listed in the ledgers aren't on the shelves.'

Niall didn't appear that interested. 'Probably somewhere else in the house,' he suggested. 'Toby did tend to leave books lying around, you know.'

'Did he? But — ' Kay was about to say in the short time since she'd arrived, it was obvious Mrs Talbot took great pride in keeping the house neat and tidy.

'But what?' Niall prompted.

She shrugged. 'Oh nothing. It doesn't matter. There's bound to be an explanation somewhere amongst all this paperwork.'

'Bound to,' Niall echoed. 'At the rate you've been working you'll be finished by the weekend.'

'Hardly that,' she chuckled. 'I've made pretty good headway in two days but there's no way I'd get through them all in a week. There are almost as many books stored on the first floor landing which Marshall had forgotten to mention. That came as a surprise, I can tell you.'

Niall smiled. 'I can imagine,' he agreed. 'They're kept at the far end, aren't they. Easy to overlook I expect.'

'Speaking of Marshall,' Kay changed the subject. 'If you've come to see him, he's had to drive to Buxton on business. He's hoping to be back around four.'

'Yes, Lucy told me.'

'Lucy?'

Niall nodded. 'She often calls my mobile. Usually to tell me her latest troubles.'

'Latest troubles?' Kay frowned. 'She seemed happy enough last night at dinner. She was looking forward to a shopping trip with her friends today.'

'Boyfriend.' Niall announced.

Kay grimaced. 'Darren. Oh, I see.'

'Whatever,' Niall shrugged. 'What's wrong with Lucy enjoying herself while she's kicking her heels around West-wood or wherever else while she's waiting for her trust fund.'

Kay's uneasiness increased. 'Let's talk about something else.'

'Just about to say the same.' Niall swung his feet back down off the table. 'I've come here to see you, not talk about the family. How about lunch?'

'Mrs Talbot said she'd be back in time to make it. You could always join me?'

'I've a better idea,' Niall swiftly dismissed the suggestion. 'There's a little pub not far from here. They do a great steak and ale pie.'

The devilish light in his blue eyes was irresistible.

'Yes, a trip out for an hour or so would be nice. I'll just get my jacket.'

'So will you be working at Westwood non-stop until you've catalogued the collection?' Niall asked over the roar of the engine as they sped off down the drive.

'Not quite.' Kay shot him a look. 'I've agreed to stay Mondays to Fridays.'

Niall gave her a sideways glance. 'Not much time for a break, Kay.'

'Oh, I'm sure I'll have the evenings off. Rachel is very capable.'

'Well, I'll be up to see Ma again soon. Maybe we could do something?'

★ ★ ★

'So can I tempt you to come in for a coffee this time?' Kay said on their return after Niall had parked his sports car outside the front door. 'It'll be my way of thanking you for such a tasty lunch.'

He checked his watch. 'Sorry,' he gave her a rueful look. 'I need to get back. Maybe next time.'

Kay felt a twinge of disappointment. 'Next time it is,' she smiled.

As she got out of the car, Niall climbed out too and walked around to her side. She began to thank him again but he cut her short.

'My pleasure,' he insisted.

Lunch with Niall had been fun. His anecdotes about the various jobs he'd done before becoming the manager of a car dealership company were hilarious.

His choice of driving the long way back to Westwood had been the perfect end to an enjoyable time and she had delighted in the rolling countryside in all its lush spring splendour.

Maybe it was being outside enjoying the beautiful spring day, or maybe it was his company, but right then the collection had lost its appeal. Yet she was loathe to admit it.

'It's not — '

The sound of a vehicle speeding up the drive was a distraction.

Kay immediately recognised the

black four by four. Marshall was back already? Unexpectedly, her heart turned over. The vehicle came to a halt in front of one of the bay windows. Moments later Marshall climbed out.

Carrying a briefcase in one hand and several folders in the other, he strode across to where they were standing.

Kay sensed rather than saw a change in Niall's demeanour. With some puzzlement, she met Marshall's cold regard.

'Kay.' He nodded a brusque greeting before turning to his cousin. 'Did you want to see me about something, Niall?'

'No, no,' Niall hastened. 'Just felt like giving the car a run.' He turned to Kay. 'Enjoyed your company, Kay.'

'Yours, too,' she responded lightly. 'Made a nice change.'

'It was a pleasure. I'll catch up with you again hopefully when our work schedules allow.'

Kay was momentarily puzzled. Hadn't they agreed over lunch to walk part of the High Peak Trail on Sunday?

Watching the two men's body language, it struck her Niall might have had his reasons for not mentioning this.

'Right then,' he turned back to Marshall, 'I'd best be off. Bye Kay.' He touched her arm briefly before walking back to the car.

'Made much progress with the collection?' Marshall asked stiffly as he opened the front door and gestured she go first.

'Yes, I have actually,' she defended firmly. The implication she'd been frittering her time with Niall was obvious.

'Of course.' His tone was icy. 'Don't let me keep you.'

With a troubled mind Kay left the charged atmosphere of the hall and walked down the corridor to the library, sensing Marshall's gaze on her back the whole time.

And as for Marshall and Niall's relationship; something definitely didn't ring right.

An hour into examining the first section of books on the centre wall, Kay frowned. Here was another discrepancy. She re-checked the ledger and Tobias's notes with the volumes in front of her.

As she stared at the page she worried her bottom lip. Things were not going so smoothly after all.

She sat up and stretched her aching back recalling Niall's suggestion the books could be somewhere else in the house. Perhaps that was it.

She had also noticed some deterioration in Tobias's handwriting for the final entries. Could a problem with his vision have meant some books had been mis-shelved?

It was feasible. Although as yet she had not found this to be the case.

At the first opportunity she would mention it to Marshall. Hopefully his mood would have improved by the time she joined him and Lucy for dinner.

★　★　★

'Peace offering?'

Kay glanced up from her notebook to see Marshall closing the library door behind him. He was carrying a tray containing two steaming mugs and a plate of biscuits.

'Hope that's tea.' His manner and expression, she noticed, had changed for the better.

'It is.'

He smiled and the bad feelings she'd been harbouring since their last conversation melted away.

She watched while he placed the tray on the work-table and pulled up a chair close to hers.

She sat back and gave him a steady look. 'Why the peace offering?'

He gave her a wry look. 'Before. When I arrived home.'

'Yes?'

'I was rather abrupt.'

'Oh, I see.'

'Of course you did but you're too polite to say so.'

She smiled, knowing she'd been

found out. 'Is that right?'

His warm expression lightened the room. 'It is.' He glanced at the paperwork in front of her. 'How's it going?'

'Slowed down a bit,' she answered lightly. 'Still, thanks to your uncle's attention to detail, it's no chore.' A frown skimmed her brow. 'Although I'm coming across some discrepancies which are proving a puzzle.'

'Discrepancies?' Marshall's dark brows rose.

'There's probably a simple answer. Some of the books listed in the ledgers are not on the shelves.'

Marshall looked puzzled. 'I find that hard to believe. Toby was meticulous about his cataloguing system. As far as I know no-one else ever read or borrowed his books. So how can that be?'

His gaze was intense, almost questioning. Immediately Kay felt on the defensive.

'See for yourself,' she said stiffly, pushing the open ledger closer to him, followed by her notepad. 'The missing books are listed here,' she added. 'Check the titles with your uncle's records then see if you can find them. I can assure you the books aren't here.'

He sensed her anger. 'Kay, I wasn't implying anything,' he insisted swiftly. He shrugged. 'It's just so unexpected.'

From his manner she could tell he was sincere and immediately felt less affronted.

'Perhaps with his health failing, it all became too much,' she suggested sympathetically. 'There's always the chance they've been shelved wrongly or been left somewhere else in the house.'

Marshall considered this for a moment. 'Can't say I recall seeing any,' he mused then read what she'd written. 'So these are the missing volumes. Now I do recognise this one.' He stabbed a finger at one of Kay's entries. '*The Naval Chronology of Great Britain*. There are three volumes in all.' He frowned. 'And a rather valuable set of books, I remember Toby saying.'

Growing troubled, Kay looked at the list again. 'Since I broke for lunch, the list has continued to grow.'

The furrows in Marshall's brow deepened. 'I'll check with Nesta. She might have seen them. And I'll search Toby's bedroom and the study. He could have put them away in a cabinet for whatever reason.'

'It's a possibility,' Kay said. 'I'll re-check his loose notes. And there's the bureau of course. There could be some bills of sale in there if he sold them on and forgot to enter it in the ledgers.'

'I'll go through the drawers now,' Marshall suggested.

Kay nodded, slightly distracted.

'There's something else,' he prompted.

She met his eyes again.

'The strange thing is, several of the missing volumes are on the list of books your uncle bequeathed to me.'

6

'Yes, we had a great time,' Lucy enthused that night over dinner. Her grey eyes, so like her brother's, sparkled as she responded to Marshall's enquiry as to how her day had gone. 'We decided on Macclesfield in the end.'

'Macclesfield?' He echoed with surprise. 'That's a fair distance from here. Then again, you've probably exhausted all the local retailers by now.'

Lucy responded to his teasing with a grimace before attacking her vegetarian lasagne again.

'We found this amazing charity shop. The prices are almost give away.'

Kay suppressed a giggle at Marshall's pained expression as his eyes sought the ceiling.

'I saw this absolutely gorgeous pink top,' Lucy chatted on, ignoring his actions. 'Mandy said it was just me and

I thought so too, so I just had to try it on and then I just had to have it and er, a few other things as well.'

From across the table, Kay couldn't help but smile. She had never see Lucy so animated.

'So you're telling me in your usual roundabout way you've already spent this month's allowance?' Marshall enquired mildly.

Kay cut into her gammon steak again, sensing Lucy was considering her response.

As she spent more time at Westwood, glimpses of the affection Marshall had for his young sister convinced her that far from being the hard individual she had first encountered, he cared deeply for the people who mattered to him.

'Well . . . yes,' Lucy admitted eventually, 'but the rest of the time is bound to fly.' She looked over at Kay for support. 'Kay, I'm sure you know how it is when you see something you know is just meant for you.'

Kay nodded. 'Of course I do,' she

encouraged. She threw Marshall a teasing smile before adding. 'Men just don't understand, do they?'

'There you are,' Lucy exclaimed triumphantly at her brother, 'I was right and you're outnumbered.'

'If that's the case,' he responded dryly, 'I'll continue to enjoy Nesta's cooking while you and Kay talk women's talk.'

After a few moments silence while everyone concentrated on their meal, Marshall brought up the subject of the missing books. 'Have you had any more thoughts about them, Lucy?' he asked.

Lucy shrugged her slender shoulders. 'I've been racking my brains trying to recall if I'd seen any but no luck, I'm afraid. Uncle Toby's books are pretty distinctive, aren't they and Mrs T wouldn't leave any lying around, particularly now . . . ' Her words tailed off, her earlier bubbliness becoming lost to an air of sadness.

Marshall turned back to Kay. 'All's not lost. There are the books on the landing. You may come across the missing volumes up there.'

'It's a possibility,' she agreed, unwilling to admit her doubts.

'I'm afraid I've some notes to finish writing up this evening,' Marshall announced following dinner when Mrs Talbot had returned to the dining room and left a pot of coffee on the sideboard for everyone to help themselves. 'Tomorrow's trip to London means an overnight stay.'

Kay felt a pang of disappointment. She had been looking forward to a relaxing evening in his company and now it looked like she wouldn't see him for the next two days.

'You work hard,' she commented.

He shrugged. 'Not as hard as I used to.'

'No,' Lucy chipped in. 'Sometimes you'd be away best part of the year.'

For a moment Marshall seemed lost to his thoughts. Kay sensed a troubled introspection about him. Then he gave his sister a small smile. 'Yes Lucy, I've a lot of time to make up for here.'

Regrets over Tobias, Kay wondered.

'That's partly what the discussions will be about tomorrow at head office,' he told them both. 'In future I shall be working more from home and spending less time abroad.'

'Is it because of me?' Lucy asked. 'I'm perfectly capable of looking after myself, you know.'

'No, Lucy,' he said softly. 'It's more a feeling of regret for a number of things. Now how's your course work going?'

Lucy pulled a face. 'OK,' she said slowly. 'Can't make up my mind about the latest ideas I've sketched.'

She turned to Kay; her enthusiasm back in place. 'Kay, would you take a look at them when you've finished your coffee and see what you think?'

Kay felt flattered. 'I'd love to. It would be interesting to compare what I did for 'A' level Art to what you're doing now.'

'You did Art, too?' Lucy exclaimed, seeing Kay in a different light.

Kay nodded. 'Yes. But books are my first love and I always wanted to join the family business. Although I still sketch and manage a few watercolours.'

'You do?' Marshall joined in.

'Yes. Mainly landscapes,' Kay answered.

'You're welcome to paint here,' Marshall suggested. 'Kinder Scout in any mood is pretty dramatic. I'd very much like to see your interpretation of it.'

'Thank you,' Kay experienced a small thrill of pleasure at his suggestion. 'I might take you up on that.'

'Please do. And now if you'll excuse me.' He finished his coffee and got to his feet. 'I must get back to my paperwork.'

Later in her room after spending time with Lucy, Kay gave up on the paperback she'd been trying to read. Lying relaxed on the top of the duvet, she stretched over and placed the book down on the bedside table.

Deciding to give Rachel a call, she swung her legs off the bed and walked over to the dressing table to pick up her mobile.

Before she'd had time to key in the number, a knock on her door was a distraction. 'Come in,' she called as she placed the phone down again.

Lucy popped her head around the door. 'Got another minute?'

'Of course,' Kay smiled, at the same time noticing Lucy's expression appeared troubled.

'Yeah,' Lucy nodded. 'The battery died on my mobile while I was trying to get hold of . . . someone, so I've had to put it on charge.'

Darren, Kay guessed. 'What about the phones downstairs?'

'Not the same and you don't know who's listening.' Lucy added darkly as she perched on the end of the bed then curled her legs beneath her. 'Oh, I don't mean anyone would deliberately listen in,' she back-peddled, seeing Kay's expression. 'I just like to keep some calls private.'

Kay sensed she wanted to get

something off her chest. 'By private I take it you mean your boyfriend?'

Lucy sighed. 'You'd like him, you know, once you got to know him. Marshall's only met him twice and straight away got this stupid idea he's a bad influence. Says a man of his age . . . ' she rolled her eyes ' . . . all of twenty-three, should know where he's going and be settled in a good career.'

Quite an age gap, Kay decided.

Lucy scowled. 'Wish I'd never brought Darren home. Wish he hadn't told Marshall he was just chilling and getting his band together when he asked what he did for a living. He's not stupid you know. He was doing a degree in economics but he dropped out.'

'Why did he drop out?'

'He was trying to find himself.'

'Oh, I see,' Kay nodded, knowing she must keep a straight face.

'Not everyone knows what they want in life the minute they leave college, do they?' Lucy defended.

'No, Lucy, I don't suppose so. But I should imagine Darren would have had the opportunity to change courses. What a pity he didn't take that option. Marshall is only concerned for your welfare.'

Lucy gave a small sound of derision. 'That's why he spent most of his time abroad earning pots of money instead. No matter what he said at dinner.' She broke off and bit her lip.

'He cares very much for you,' Kay said softly. 'Try to remember that.'

Sensing she was about to lose the young girl's confidence, Kay said. 'Give him a chance, Lucy. He did say he was intending to spend more time at Westwood.'

'Probably to check up on me,' Lucy sulked. 'Still once I leave for uni, I'll be able to do as I please.'

Despite her comment, Kay could see this reminder about Marshall's future plans had set Lucy thinking.

'Why can't he be like Niall,' she sighed. 'He's much more fun even though he has Auntie Helen to worry about.'

Kay woke early the next morning but not early enough to see Marshall before he left.

When Mrs Talbot explained her husband had driven him to the station an hour previously, Kay hid her disappointment at not being able to tell him of last night's talk with Lucy. She was sure this would have taken some of the worry off his mind.

'Morning, Kay.' Lucy dashed into the dining room, poured herself some fresh orange juice then quickly pulled out a chair. She snatched a piece of toast from the toast-rack and quickly buttered it.

'No time for anything else, sorry Mrs T,' she said as the housekeeper came into the room.

'Today's a half-day, isn't it?' Mrs Talbot checked.

'Yes, I'll be back just after one.'

'Well you can make up for it then. I'll see you have a decent lunch.'

'OK.' Lucy took a bite of toast. 'Anything for a quiet life,' she added quietly to Kay. Toast in hand, Lucy pushed back her chair. 'I'll have to dash,' she said. 'Bus is due any minute. See you later, Kay!'

Determined to make the most of the day, Kay set to work in the library and soon became absorbed in checking the last section of shelving before planning to move on to the books on the landing.

She was almost finished when her mobile rang. It was Lucy.

Instinctively Kay checked her watch and was surprised to see it was almost one o'clock.

'Hi, Kay,' Lucy enthused. 'Just a quickie. Last night Marshall did say he'd be away until tomorrow, didn't he?'

Something in Lucy's tone sent alarm bells ringing.

'Yes, he did,' she answered cautiously. 'Is there something you need to speak to him about?'

'No. Not really.'

'Then why — '

'Oh, it's nothing,' Lucy interrupted. 'It's just that Darren's giving me a lift home.'

Kay's heart sank.

'I've got a stack of CDs for him, that's all. We're on our way now. Just wanted to make sure the coast was clear.'

Kay's unease increased. 'Lucy, are you sure — '

'Course I am. It's not like he'll be staying for the rest of the day. I've got course work to do.'

'I see,' Kay said, thankful to hear this. If Darren was only dropping Lucy off, surely Marshall wouldn't be too angry when he heard. Which he was bound to. 'I'll see you both shortly then.'

Ending the call, Kay's mood remained pensive. After a moment or two, she'd made up her mind to be in the hall when Lucy and Darren arrived.

Under the pretext of wanting to chat, she decided she would keep Darren talking while Lucy fetched the CDs from her room.

She left the library and went into the main sitting room at the front of the house to watch for their arrival. Partly obscured by the heavy brocade drapes, Kay looked out of the window where she could see a fair way down the drive.

Moments later a dark blue van raced up towards the house and screeched to a halt outside the bay, sending a spray of gravel over the flower beds.

Even from inside the sitting room, Kay could hear loud thudding music assaulting the peace of the gardens. First impressions, she concluded, had her thinking the same as Marshall.

Then the engine was cut and the music died. As soon as she saw both doors fly open, she hurried from the room. She had just entered the hall when the front door opened.

'Kay,' Lucy greeted happily. 'Thought you'd still be in the library. I was just going to bring Darren through to meet you. Darren,' she turned to her companion, her eyes shining, 'this is my friend, Kay. She's working on Uncle Toby's books. Remember, I told you all about it last week.'

'Yeah?' Darren couldn't have looked less interested.

Kay's mind was made up. Marshall was right not to be enamoured of him she decided meeting his sullen gaze.

While there was nothing particularly wrong in his appearance; not a gelled hair out of place and his sunbed tan perfection, he appeared vain and unforthcoming.

For someone who was 'still finding himself' she couldn't help but wonder how he could afford so many gold chains and what appeared to be a Rolex watch.

'Oh, you're useless, Darren,' Lucy chuckled, slipping her arm through his and pulling him to her.

'Had enough of books at uni,' he responded ungraciously. 'Music's where it's at.'

Kay jumped at the opportunity.

'Lucy, isn't that why Darren's here? The CDs,' she prompted with a smile before turning again to the boyfriend. 'You can tell me who's the latest big thing while Lucy gets them.'

7

When Marshall returned Friday evening, Kay knew she would have to mention Darren's visit as there was every possibility of something being said by the Talbots while she was away for the weekend.

Not having had the opportunity to see Marshall before dinner, Kay was still wondering how to go about breaking the news when she joined him and Lucy in the dining-room.

During the first course she was aware Lucy was being particularly reticent whenever Marshall attempted conversation.

Kay glanced across the table. Is she annoyed with me, she wondered, or sulking over Darren's swift departure once he had been given the discs the night before.

It was clear to Kay that his off-hand, 'See ya' to Lucy was a lot less than she was expecting. She felt sorry for the young girl; her hurt feelings had been so clearly defined in her face.

'You're quiet tonight, Lucy.' Marshall eventually said.

Lucy put down her knife and fork and shrugged. 'I've a lot on my mind.' Seeing Marshall's frown she shot a look of uncertainty at Kay before addressing her brother again. 'Course work,' she hastened. ' 'A' Levels, remember?'

She's worried I'm going to mention Darren, Kay guessed. But now was not the time.

'If your sketches are anything to go by,' she encouraged, 'I'm sure you've nothing to worry about.'

Lucy didn't look convinced. 'Thank you,' she said quietly. 'Marshall, if you don't mind, I'd like to go up to my room now. I've more studying to do.'

'But you've hardly touched your meal,' he complained.

'I'm fine, honestly.' She gave him a wan smile and got up from the table. 'Will you be around in the morning?'

'Yes. From now on, I'll be here for most of the time.'

'You will?' Lucy looked surprised. And despite the tiredness etching her features, Kay sensed this news pleased her.

The same pleasure, she judged, that was flooding through her at hearing the news.

'D'you have time for coffee, Kay?' Marshall asked when the meal was over. 'Or do you need to get off straight away?'

Kay's conscience told her she would have to mention Darren's visit before she left.

'I'm in no great hurry,' she said.

'Good. Let's take it in the sitting-room,' He gave her a satisfied look. 'After a hectic round of business meetings and travel, I just want to relax.'

'Fine by me,' she smiled. 'I'll bring the tray through.'

'Any luck with the missing books?' Marshall asked once they were settled in the sitting-room in front of the fire.

Kay shook her head. 'No luck at all,'

she sighed. 'But at least the list hasn't grown any longer since I started on the books upstairs. The count still remains at fifteen.'

For a moment, Marshall appeared lost in thought. 'Well, I suppose that's something to be thankful for. Although it troubles me that it includes some of the books you've been promised. If they don't turn up, you'll have to choose alternatives.'

'I wouldn't dream of it,' Kay protested. 'Your uncle was more than generous. I'd have been very happy with just one book as a memento of happier times.'

'Your heart's in the right place, Kay,' he said.

His compliment warmed her from top to toe.

'You miss him very much, don't you?'

'Terribly,' he admitted. 'Still, at least he didn't suffer. I don't know whether it's been mentioned, but Nesta found him in his favourite armchair in the library with one of his books open on his knees. Said he looked like he'd just fallen asleep.'

Then he appeared to snap out of his thoughts. 'But that's all in the past now. So, d'you have any plans for the weekend?'

'Nothing special,' she said, immediately feeling a rush of guilt for not mentioning her date with Niall on Sunday. To do so, she sensed, would spoil the intimacy of this time together. 'I'll need to catch up with what's been happening in the shop, of course.'

He gave her a wry look. 'Not much of a break then. Maybe I could take you out for dinner Saturday night or lunch on Sunday?'

'I'm seeing Rachel, Saturday night.' She looked down at her coffee cup. It was too late now to say, and actually I've just remembered I'm seeing your cousin on Sunday.

'It's all right, Kay. I didn't mean to embarrass you.'

She looked up quickly. His expression was inscrutable.

'You're not embarrassing me. It's just that — ' she hedged.

'Some things take priority over others. I understand.'

That wasn't what she was thinking at all but as an explanation it would have to do.

Once more his eyes held hers as he changed the subject.

'How has Lucy been these last two days? Did you manage to have a chat with her?'

'Yes,' Kay smiled. 'Several in fact.'

Marshall looked amused. 'Sounds like my sister.'

'She's a lovely girl, Marshall. I'm sure everything is going to be fine.' A shadow crossed Kay's face. 'There was just one thing.'

As Marshall's brow frowned, she prepared herself for some angry words.

'Darren dropped Lucy off from college the day you travelled down to London. He was only here for a matter of minutes,' she hastened as Marshall's mouth became one tight line. 'She had some CDs for him. That was all. She spent the rest of the day on her course work.'

Marshall placed his cup and saucer on the low table between their two chairs and Kay could see his mind was racing.

'If you could only reassure her how much she means to you, rather than being so authoritative,' she blurted before she could stop herself, 'I'm sure she would take it onboard and see things differently.'

Kay worried her bottom lip. Had she said too much? Overstepped the mark? After all, it was barely two weeks since she'd first encountered Tobias's family.

'I wish I had your confidence, Kay,' Marshall sighed. 'Still, it's worth a try. I'll talk to her over the weekend.'

Kay relaxed again. 'You won't regret it,' she said softly. She placed her cup down on the table. 'And now I'd best be off.'

'D'you have much to bring down to your car?' Marshall asked as they both got to their feet.

'Not really. Just a few things.'

'In that case, I'll give you a hand. No point in bothering Jack now.'

When Marshall saw Kay's two suitcases at the foot of her bed, he raised a brow. 'You are coming back, aren't you? Seems rather a lot just for the weekend.'

She smiled at his expression, happy his mood had lightened. 'It's mainly washing,' she explained. 'I can't expect Mrs Talbot to do it for me. And yes, I'll be back first thing Monday morning.'

'I'm pleased to hear it.'

'Oh and I've taken the ledgers again,' she remembered. 'If I can find the time, I'll do a little more work on them. Keep up the momentum.'

He gave her a wry look. 'I thought this was a weekend break.'

'It's only if I find the time,' she repeated with a smile.

How different he now seemed to the hostile person she'd first encountered, she reflected as Marshall carried her cases downstairs.

She paused for a moment before getting into the driver's seat. 'I'll see you Monday. I hope your talk with Lucy goes well.'

'I hope so, too. Hurry back, Kay.'

He smiled and something touched her heart.

'I will,' she said, hoping she didn't sound as breathless as she was feeling.

He waited until she was settled in her seat then closed the car door, his warm expression had her wishing she was not going home after all.

The first stars were appearing in the pale sky as she passed through the village and continued up the climbing, twisting road and the eventual open moorland.

Her thoughts full of Marshall, she was not prepared for a particularly sharp bend suddenly looming in front of her. She hit the brakes and quickly changed gear. Then mindful of his reminder to drive carefully, she reduced her speed to a safer pace.

As the road climbed further still, the twinkling lights of an occasional farmhouse nestling in the dark folds of the hills was the only hint she was not alone on the moor.

Then the sudden glare of headlights in the near distance came as an unwelcome surprise. With a sharp exclamation Kay dipped her own, expecting the other driver to do the same. But as the gap narrowed between them she had the feeling this was not going to happen.

Annoyance turned to concern as the oncoming brightness lit up the interior of her car. Then came the chilling realisation that the approaching vehicle was dangerously over on her side of the road and showing no sign of slowing down.

Blinded by the increasing glare, self-preservation swiftly took over.

Heart racing, she frantically turned the steering wheel to avoid a collision. As the car pitched forward at an alarming angle she knew she had lost control.

8

'It's all right, love. We've got you.' Somewhere beyond the realm of consciousness, Kay became aware of the distant sound of voices.

A sudden cold blast of air was a shock to her system but the male voice remained comfortably reassuring.

She tried to focus her eyes against an unsteady light. Then she remembered Tobias's ledgers.

'My bag?' she whispered.

'Don't fret about that. We'll find it for you. I'm Dave ... Dave Fletcher, paramedic. My partner, Steve, is holding the torch but he's not making a very good job of it in this wind, is he? Now don't worry, we'll soon have you out. What's your name, sweetheart?'

'Kay ... Deacon,' she managed. Her mouth felt as dry as a desert, and every part of her was beginning to hurt.

'Good girl. Right Kay, I want you to keep perfectly still while I fix this collar around your neck. There we go. You did that perfectly. Now can you feel your feet? Good. Wriggle your toes?'

Concentrating hard, it seemed easier to manage this with her right foot. She pressed it against what she imagined to be the floor of the car. 'Yes, this one . . . the right.'

'Excellent. Now how about the left?'

She struggled for a moment. 'Not so well,' she gasped. 'There seems to be a weight pressing on it.'

'Let's take a look then. Steve?' Dave directed.

As Steve pointed the torch further into the car's floor space, Dave leaned further in. 'Ah, what have we got here? Think it's that bag you were talking about, Kay.'

The next moment Kay felt the pressure ease.

'Try it now.' Dave encouraged.

'That's better,' she whispered. 'I can move it.'

'Now can you grip my hand?'

She did as instructed.

'No worries there then,' he grinned. 'But we'll have you checked out in hospital just to be on the safe side.'

It was a relief to be lying inside the ambulance in safe hands as they sped towards the local hospital.

Then Kay remembered the ledgers. Eyes wide she looked across at Dave sitting facing her. 'My bag,' she gasped 'It's not still in the car, is it?'

'What is it with you women and your bags,' he exclaimed light-heartedly. 'Don't worry. We've got it here.' He held it up for her to see. 'And judging by the weight, I don't think you could get another thing inside. Bad as my missus.'

Relief swept over her. 'Can I just see inside?'

Dave raised the flap and held it so she had a clear view.

The four ledgers were intact.

'Happy?'

She settled back on the pillow again. 'Yes,' she sighed. 'Thank you.'

'And don't even think about coming downstairs,' Rachel ordered late the following morning after driving Kay home from the hospital. 'Ginny and Peter are looking after the shop. You can take it easy on the sofa while I make you a drink.'

'But I'm fine.' Kay insisted as Rachel swept off into the kitchen, keeping the truth to herself that she still felt somewhat shaky after her ordeal. 'I've been checked from top to toe,' she called after her. 'No broken bones, no concussion, just some bruising. I'll stiffen up if I lie around doing nothing.'

Her protests ignored, she wandered over to the window and looked out across the busy town square at the shop fronts opposite.

'Drink it while it's hot.' Behind her, Rachel continued to play at being mother. Kay walked back to the sofa and sat down gingerly.

'And don't give me any more frights

like that,' Rachel said as she handed Kay her drink then made herself comfortable in an armchair.

Sensing the concern she was disguising, Kay gave her a smile. 'I didn't do it on purpose.'

'No,' Rachel said, 'I know you didn't.' Then her expression hardened. 'But from what you've told me, it sounds very much like the idiot in the other vehicle did.'

Kay's blood ran cold at the thought. 'But why would someone do that?'

Rachel shrugged, verging momentarily on the tearful, knowing Kay had had such a lucky escape. 'Who knows,' she sniffed. 'It was probably a boy racer trying to impress his mates or a girlfriend.'

'You're probably right,' Kay sighed. 'And now thanks to whoever it was, I'm without a car until the insurance company gives the go ahead to hire one.'

'Keith will probably recover your car.' Rachel interrupted Kay's troubled thoughts. 'His garage deals with most of the wrecks around here.'

'Let's hope he thinks it's worth repairing.'

'Are you still going to carry on with the collection?' Rachel asked. 'Maybe you should take some time off.'

'I'd rather carry on. It's not difficult. I'll get on to my insurance in a minute, then I'll have to phone Marshall. Tell him what's happened. Hopefully he'll offer to pick me up Sunday evening.'

'Keith and I could always take you back if he can't manage it,' Rachel suggested. 'After what's happened, I'd rather he did the driving.'

'That would be — '

Kay's response was cut short by the buzz of the internal phone her father had had fitted many years ago.

'It's all right, Rachel, I'll see to it,' she said as Rachel began to get up.

Kay reached over to the side table and picked up the receiver. 'Yes, Ginny?'

'I have a Mr Garner here. He's

asking for you. Are you free to see him?'

Kay's heart turned over. 'Yes, of course. Please tell him I'll be down in a minute.'

Kay replaced the receiver and turned to Rachel. 'Marshall's here. I wonder if he's heard about the accident. Although I can't see how.'

She winced as she attempted to get up from the sofa.

Rachel was quick to notice. 'See, I said you won't be able to carry on as though nothing's happened. Wouldn't it be better if you saw him here?'

Kay had a change of heart. 'You're right. It would. Will you show him up for me?'

A few moments later when Marshall walked into the sitting room, the pleasure at seeing him so soon again evaporated. The strain on his face had her wondering what else had happened.

'Kay?' He looked at her for what seemed an age before coming over to where she was sitting. 'You're all right?'

So he had heard. News travelled fast.

For some reason she suddenly felt very tearful and wanted his arms around her.

Blinking furiously, she gave him a small smile. 'Yes, apart from some bruising, I'm fine.'

The relief on his face was uplifting. Could it be his feelings were beginning to match her own? Suddenly it all became too much for her.

He frowned. 'You're upset.'

She snatched a tissue from the box on the table and blew her nose. 'Probably delayed shock,' she sniffed. 'Please, sit down.'

Then before she knew it, the tears started falling.

'Oh, Kay,' he groaned.

The next moment she was experiencing the wonderful sensation of being wrapped in his arms. And was that really the soft touch of his lips brushing her temple or her desires placing them there?

'If you'd been badly hurt,' he said softly, 'I don't know how I'd have lived with myself.'

Reluctantly she came out of her dreams and through glistening eyes focused on his strained expression.

'But why,' she whispered. 'It was no fault of yours.'

There was tension in his body while she waited for his response.

'No,' he agreed. 'It's just that . . . '

She met his gaze which she could see held a hint of uncertainty. Was it possible for Marshall to be stuck for words?

' . . . in such a short time you've made a big difference in our lives,' he began again. 'Talking to Lucy earlier this morning, it was clear you've already influenced her way of thinking.'

Kay's dreams dissolved in an instant. So really, it was all about Lucy.

'That's very flattering.' She wriggled free and edged away, disguising her disappointment by the appearance of wanting to dispose of the tissue.

'You're really sure you're OK?' Marshall asked again after she had dropped it in the waste basket.

'Yes, I'm certain. I had a thorough examination at the hospital and an overnight stay, then Rachel drove me home. So how did you get to hear?'

'I was driving into town and recognised your car. It had just been winched up on to the road by the recovery wagon.' His eyes looked troubled again. 'What on earth happened, Kay?'

She recounted the cause of the accident. 'But don't worry, the ledgers weren't damaged,' she added. 'They're over there on the bureau.'

'I'm not worried about the ledgers,' he retorted with a force that surprised her. 'I'm concerned about what happened to you.' His grey gaze was intense. 'You have reported this to the police, haven't you? Whoever drove you off the road is a lunatic and shouldn't be behind a wheel.'

'It was suggested at the hospital that I contact the police,' she said, 'but I'm in two minds whether to bother or not. I couldn't give a description of the vehicle or say whether the driver was male or female.'

'Your insurance company will probably need to know if the police were notified when you fill in your claim form,' Marshall said.

Kay frowned. 'Will they? I've never had to deal with anything like this before.' She paused. 'I can't be certain but I think the other vehicle was a transit van . . . blue or black.'

'Well that's something you can tell them,' Marshall insisted.

Kay made up her mind. 'I'll give them a call later.'

'Good.' Marshall looked satisfied. 'You'll be pleased to hear your car doesn't appear to be too badly damaged.'

'That is good news,' she sighed.

'You were lucky, Kay. Really lucky. The farmer's gate saved you. A few feet either way and you'd have hit the wall.' Marshall shook his head and left his thoughts unsaid. 'Once you feel up to carrying on with the cataloguing, I'll drive you.'

She sensed the offer was his attempt to stop her dwelling on what might have happened and she appreciated it.

She smiled. 'As I've just been telling Rachel, I feel fine now.'

He looked at her admiringly. 'Are you sure?'

'Perfectly. The collection will be a distraction to my troubles.'

'In that case I could pick you up early Sunday evening. We'd be back home in time for dinner.'

Back home. If he only knew how sweet those two words sounded. For the second time she closed the door on her dreams. 'Yes,' she said, 'I'd like that.'

'And how's the bookshop going?'

'Business as usual,' she was happy to say. 'So no worries there.'

Marshall checked his watch. 'I'll leave you to get some rest.' Concern shadowed his face again. 'Now you will contact the police?'

'Yes, promise,' she agreed.

'Good. Would you like me to ring tomorrow before I drive over. Just in case you have a change of heart?'

'Ring by all means,' Kay agreed happily. 'But the way I'm feeling now, I'll be packed and ready to leave by six.'

9

'Thought I'd been stood up,' Niall greeted with an expression of relief when Kay opened the door. He glanced back down towards the car park. 'Your car's not there.'

Of course Niall wouldn't know about her near-miss.

'Hi, Niall,' she smiled. 'Come in. It's off the road for the time being,' she added as he wiped his feet and stepped into the narrow hallway. 'Had a bit of a near miss Friday night on my way back from Westwood.'

Niall's good humour faded. 'No! What happened?'

Kay hesitated. She didn't want to dwell on the experience. 'Nothing much to tell, really. Took the top road back and in the darkness somehow ended up in a farmer's field.'

'What!' Niall regarded her in disbelief. 'You were lucky. Some of the fields round here border on the vertical. That must have been hairy.'

'You could say that.' Kay gave him a wry look.

Niall followed her through.

'We could do this some other time you know.'

'I'm fine,' she insisted. 'A walk should take away the stiffness I'm feeling. Although I don't think I'll be able to manage more than a mile or two.'

'Hey, I wasn't planning on walking that far,' he teased. 'Well,' he grinned, 'if you're ready, let's go burn some rubber.'

Her expression had a sobering effect. 'What am I saying.' He raised his palms in defence. 'I'll take it easy, promise.'

'See you do,' she smiled.

True to his word, Niall drove over the hills and through the valleys at a reasonable speed.

Soon Kay was enjoying their stroll along part of the Parsley Hay section of the High Peak Trail. At times it felt like they had it to themselves, with only an occasional walker to greet.

'Mind if we call it a day now?' she asked.

'Not at all,' Niall agreed. 'Let's find the nearest pub and have a drink'

'D'you mind if we drive straight back,' Kay asked, feeling slightly troubled that each time they met, a pub always featured. 'I'm going back to Westwood this evening and I've some packing to do before Marshall picks me up.'

Niall's easy mood faded. 'Already? You shouldn't be going back just yet. He's cracking the whip, Kay. I wouldn't have it.'

'It's not like that at all,' she exclaimed. 'I was the one to insist on continuing.'

'A case of the sooner it's done the better. Is that it?' He looked at her for a long moment.

More of a case of wanting to be around Marshall, the small voice of truth added but she'd never admit that for the world.

'You don't seem so sure.'

Kay was beginning to feel annoyed by Niall's prying attitude.

'I can't take too much time away from work,' she shrugged.

She broke the growing awkwardness between them. 'Let's not spoil a pleasant walk, Niall.'

'You're right,' he smiled, taking her hand in his. 'Let's get you home.'

'You know we're going to have to do this again,' he said later as they entered the square and drove past the book-shop.

Kay threw him a glance. Why didn't this please her, she wondered, then answered her own question. Despite Niall's lively, fun-loving attitude to life, he would never be the man his cousin was.

In the short time she'd spent at Westwood, her judgement of Marshall had been turned on its head. She accepted she'd fallen in love with him but she doubted he felt the same.

'Kay?'

'Sorry,' she frowned glancing at him.

'We are going to see more of each other, aren't we?'

'Maybe . . . when I've got my life back together again.'

'Oh, right.' Niall shot her a look as he slowed down to take the corner into the side road. 'That sounds very much like the brush off.'

Moments later he brought the car to a halt in one of the parking bays. He released the seatbelt and swivelled round. As he placed his arm on the back of her seat, she'd never seen him look so serious. 'There's someone else on the scene?'

'It's not that,' she denied.

'No?' Niall was quick to pick up. 'You took just a little too long to answer. That means there is and I get the feeling it's recent.'

His blue eyes raked her face with such intensity she had to look away.

'No,' he breathed. 'Don't tell me you've fallen for that grim cousin of mine.'

Kay knew the colour flooding into her face was betraying her. 'As I said before, I've a lot on my hands at the moment, Niall,' she floundered. 'I've no time for a relationship.'

'You're sure about that?'

She met his gaze again and tried to ignore his sarcasm. 'Perfectly.'

All at once she didn't want to be with him any more. 'I must go.' She reached for her bag at her feet. 'I've packing to do. Thanks for today. I feel so much better for the exercise.'

She turned to get out of the car but he was too fast for her.

Before she knew what was happening she was gripped in a vice-like hold and he was kissing her. With some effort, she managed to twist her face away. 'Niall, please,' she gasped.

He released her. 'Never force a lady,' she heard him say as she fumbled with the door. 'Here, let me.'

She shrank back into the seat as he leaned across and released the lock. As soon as she was able she unfastened her seat belt then pushed against the door, relieved to feel it open.

'You can't blame a guy for trying, Kay. No hard feelings?'

His smile begged forgiveness. Maybe she had reacted too strongly, she decided. 'No hard feelings,' she agreed as she got out and closed the passenger door.

Seconds later Niall reversed out of the space. Tyres squealing, he disappeared around the corner just as Marshall's four-by-four turned into the car park.

Kay's stomach turned over. There was no way the two men could have missed seeing each other.

She quickly checked her watch, disbelieving the time could have gone so quickly. She was right. Marshall was early.

As he pulled into the space Niall had just vacated, a glimpse of the grim line of his jaw told her he had clearly seen his cousin.

She sighed as she slipped her bag on

to her shoulder, convinced the day was going to end on a sour note.

'Hello, Marshall,' she greeted him after he had swung out of the vehicle. Then she made a point of looking at her watch. 'I wasn't expecting you so soon.'

'Good to see my cousin's nothing special,' he said, ignoring her comment.

Kay frowned.

'Friday evening,' he prompted. 'You said you had nothing special planned for the weekend. Now I know what it was.'

Heat seared her cheeks. Anger or embarrassment, she wasn't sure. She got straight to the point.

'There's some animosity between you and Niall, isn't there. But don't make me part of it. He's entertaining and I've enjoyed his company, but that's as far as it goes.'

The tension appeared to leave Marshall's body as he looked down at her. 'I'm sorry, Kay,' he sighed. 'You're right to be angry. Who you choose to befriend is none of my business. I just don't want to see you get hurt.'

Emotion closed her throat. The only man who had the ability to hurt her feelings would never know it.

Other than acting as some kind of temporary guiding light to Lucy, she reflected miserably, she mattered very little in his life.

'If you prefer, I'll wait out here until you're ready to leave,' he said.

'No, I don't prefer.' She pulled herself together then attempted to lighten the mood. 'You'll accuse me of being unsociable next. Come up to the flat. Everything's more or less packed. I won't keep you waiting long.'

She went to turn away and felt his hand on her shoulder.

'Kay?'

The next moment she was in his arms experiencing the hard strength of his body against hers. 'I always get it wrong.' His breath stirred against her hair. 'I'm such a fool.'

She raised her head and met his eyes.

'That's one thing you'll never be.'

A short time later and never feeling happier, Kay accompanied Marshall across the car park where he loaded her cases into his vehicle.

'How's Lucy?' she asked after she'd clipped her seatbelt in place and Marshall pulled away. 'She texted me last night asking if there was anything she could do to help. It was sweet of her.'

'She's fine,' Marshall replied. He gave her a quick smile before concentrating on the road again. 'She was shocked when I got home and told her about the accident. Asking me to bring her over there and then but when I explained you were insisting on carrying on with the collection, she calmed down again.'

Kay was touched by Lucy's concern.

'She wanted to come out with me today,' he added, 'but a friend's birthday has been planned for some time. She'll see you when she gets back.'

'I'll look forward to it,' Kay said.

'D'you mind if I take the top road?' Marshall asked a short while later when they weren't far from the turn off. 'It's the most direct one but of course it means passing the spot where you came off.'

'No, I don't mind,' Kay agreed.

She had been anticipating the inevitable with some apprehension, but with Marshall at her side and their relationship blossoming, it made the prospect a whole lot easier. 'As I've no idea where it happened, I'll remain in blissful ignorance.'

She was rewarded with an admiring look. 'OK. Just don't be on the lookout for a broken farm gate.'

Many miles on and Kay wished she'd kept her word. Dark skid marks on the road surface up ahead had her putting two and two together. The closer they got to them, morbid curiosity took over.

Like a moth drawn to a flame, she looked out of the side window. Far below, scattered pieces of a wooden gate looked like broken matchsticks.

The enormity of her narrow escape struck home. She drew breath as a feeling of dizziness threatened to overcome her. She leaned back in the seat and closed her eyes.

'Blast,' she heard Marshall exclaim.

She was aware of him swiftly changing gear and bringing the vehicle to a halt then felt the gentle touch of his hand on her shoulder.

'Kay?'

She opened her eyes to meet the concern in his.

'Are you all right?'

She nodded.

'I never expected — ' she broke off.

Marshall looked grim. 'It was thoughtless of me to come this way so soon after the event. You didn't need that.'

The rest of the week passed all too swiftly for Kay and by Friday afternoon her work was done. There was disappointment each time she had added yet another title to the list of missing books and found no trace of the others.

But the time spent with Marshall and

Lucy more than compensated her frustrations at not being able to solve this mystery.

'Am I right in thinking you're almost done?'

Kneeling down at a bottom shelf, Kay looked up to see Marshall coming down the landing.

'Just finished,' she confirmed. 'But sad to say the list of missing books has increased.'

A frown scored her brow. He shook his head. 'I just don't understand it. Are any of the latest ones part of your bequest?'

Kay shook her head. 'Not this time. I've added them to the list. Take a look.' She picked up a sheet of lined paper and handed it to him.

Looking grim, Marshall scrutinised it. 'I just don't know how we're going to get to the bottom of this.'

'That's why I've made a copy for myself,' Kay said, 'if that's all right with you.'

'Of course,' he agreed but his

puzzlement as to why she should want to do this was in his expression.

'I've been thinking of ringing round my contacts in the book trade,' she explained. 'If any of the books came up for sale over the last twelve months or so there will be a record of them. Besides, your uncle was such a distinctive character, he would be easily remembered.'

'It's possible, I suppose,' Marshall decided. For a moment he appeared lost in thought. 'And a satisfactory conclusion. Don't forget to choose alternatives to the ones you were promised,' he added. 'Whatever you feel is appropriate.'

'Really, Marshall, I — ' She broke off. His expression told her to argue would be pointless. 'Thank you. That's very kind.'

'The rest of your bequest? Am I right in thinking the books are still here?'

'Yes, they are.'

And here they belong, she decided.

'Would you like me to help you box

them up? I'm sure Nesta or Jack would be able to provide something to carry them in.'

She knew if she revealed her feelings about the collection remaining intact, Marshall would not hear of it. For the time being she would let him think she was going ahead with his wishes.

'D'you mind if we leave it for now? Time's getting on and I was hoping to see Rachel before she closes for the day. We could always arrange a date once I'm on top of things at the shop.'

He gave her a long look. 'Any day, any time. Whichever you prefer. Now I expect you're ready to leave.'

It was the last thing she wanted. Time spent in his company was precious.

'Yes, of course,' she answered.

'It won't seem the same not having you here working on the collection.'

Marshall's expression was thoughtful and for a moment she was tempted to say how much she was going to miss him. But it wouldn't do to wear her heart on her sleeve.

'And I'll miss being here, too,' she said.

Fearful her eyes would betray her feelings, she turned away and gathered up her things off the small table she'd been using.

'Then you will have to come again,' he smiled. 'You'll do that?'

'Of course.'

He looked pleased with her answer. 'Let's arrange a date on the drive back to town.'

Kay matched his smile. 'Yes, let's. I'll just say goodbye to Lucy before we go,' she remembered. 'Oh, and I must thank Mrs Talbot, too.'

They parted at the end of the landing. Marshall headed downstairs while Kay took the other staircase up to her room.

For the last time, she looked around the tasteful cream and apricot décor and furnishings now so familiar to her, then quickly set to work packing her belongings.

'You're leaving already,' Lucy complained after Kay explained she had come to say goodbye. She got up from her desk and wrapped her arms around her. 'This is awful,' she sighed. 'I'm going to miss you so much.'

'Me, too,' Kay said, resurfacing from Lucy's tight hug. 'But I'll be back and you must call in the shop whenever you're in town.'

'Too right,' Lucy agreed with feeling.

'And when you get your results, we'll do something special to celebrate.'

Lucy pulled a face. 'I wish I had your confidence.'

'You'll be fine,' Kay assured her. 'If there's anything you need to talk about, promise you'll give me a ring.'

'I will,' Lucy sniffed, her eyes filling. 'You'll be sorry you offered.'

'I'd best be off then.' Kay gave her a last hug. 'Marshall's waiting to drive me back.'

Moments later as she walked downstairs, the phone in the hall began to ring; something she'd come to realise happened continually when Marshall was home.

As she placed her suitcase near the front door, she hoped this time it wasn't for him.

The radio was playing softly when she walked into the kitchen. Nesta was cutting out some scones on a floured board while Marshall was speaking on the kitchen extension at the far end of the room.

He broke the call when he saw Kay and placed his hand over the mouthpiece.

'Something's cropped up at head office,' he explained. 'Sorry Kay, it looks like I'm going to be tied up for the rest of the afternoon. Jack will drive you home.'

10

During the lunch-time lull, Kay had just finished dealing with a customer when she was surprised and delighted to see Lucy coming into the shop.

These feelings were short lived when she saw Darren follow her in. 'And don't be long,' she heard him instruct. 'I've got things to do.'

Kay's hackles began to rise. What Lucy saw in him remained an utter mystery. She shot an icy look in his direction.

With a frown, Darren turned away and began to browse the shelves at the far end of the shop.

'Men,' Lucy exclaimed, seeing Kay's expression. 'They all hate shopping, don't they? And don't fret, Marshall isn't going to come in and catch us. He's away on business again. He'll never know I skipped college this morning.'

Kay frowned. 'Oh, Lucy, you haven't!'

'Stop worrying,' Lucy dismissed. 'I don't make a habit of it. Anyway, officially it's my lunch break now. Darren wants to call into the music store next. I'm buying him some CDs before he drops me off at college.'

Concern for Marshall's sister still on her mind, yet loathe to interfere, Kay made no further comment on the couple being together, seemingly behind Marshall's back.

'Marshall's keeping busy, then?'

Lucy nodded. 'Almost like he used to because of some crisis or other at head office. Although,' she lowered her voice, 'to be honest, I'm glad he's away at the moment. Not because of Darren,' she hastened, 'but since last week there's been no pleasing him. What it's about, I haven't a clue.'

'Must be the business,' Kay suggested.

'Never seemed to bother him before and he was doing twice as much then. Anyway enough of him,' Lucy grinned,

'I've come to see you. Have you anything I could get some ideas from for fabric designs? Like something from nature.'

Kay considered Lucy's request for a moment. 'You could be spoilt for choice. We've several books of nature photography in stock at the moment; here and abroad. They're over on the far side.'

A short time later Kay bagged the book Lucy had decided upon.

'See you soon,' Lucy said cheerfully before going over to Darren. 'See, I didn't take long, did I?' Kay heard her say.

With no response other than a sullen look in Kay's direction, Darren turned and walked out of the shop without saying a word.

As the couple disappeared past the window, Kay's worried look did not go unnoticed by Rachel.

'I take it that was Tobias's niece,' she said as she joined her behind the counter.

Kay nodded. 'Yes, that's Lucy.'

'Seems a bubbly, pretty young thing. Pity about the boyfriend.'

'You noticed his manner,' Kay said. 'Marshall would be furious if he knew she was spending time with him instead of being in college.'

'Best not get involved.'

'I know,' Kay sighed. 'But I'm very fond of Lucy.'

'Well, there's nothing you can do about it. Apart from checking on those missing books, you're not concerned with the family any more.'

Rachel's off-hand remark was like a knife twisting in Kay's heart. If only she knew how she felt about Marshall.

She tried to resign herself to the situation. Moping around wasn't the way to run a business.

Seated at her desk, the list of missing books in front of her, Kay picked up the receiver and punched in the number of the next specialist bookshop to be checked.

'*Naval Chronology of Great Britain*,'

the owner of a Sheffield bookshop repeated after Kay had mentioned the title. 'It just so happens I got my hands on a copy last week.'

Kay's heart turned over. She couldn't believe her luck. A positive response on only her third call.

'You did, Mr Jackson,' she exclaimed. 'All three volumes?'

'No, more's the pity. Seller only had one. I told him I'd been keen to buy the other two, so he said he'd see what he could do. Seemed positive enough,' Hector Jackson continued. 'Promised to get back to me soon.'

Kay took a breath. 'Mr Jackson, I'm sorry to have to tell you this but there's the chance these books were stolen from a collection I recently catalogued.'

'Stolen!'

Kay swiftly moved the receiver from her ear as Hector Jackson's exclamation reverberated down the line. At the same time Rachel popped her head around the office door, then seeing Kay was busy, disappeared again.

'Now, Kay, you and your father have known me for — '

'Of course we have,' she interrupted. 'It goes without saying you bought the book in good faith. Besides, it might not even be one of the volumes I'm trying to trace.'

'And how are we to judge that?'

'Do you have the book there?'

'Just give me a minute.'

Anticipation was almost unbearable as Kay waited for Hector to come back on the line. If the book did turn out to be Tobias's copy, how had it got into another person's hands? Had there been a burglary at Westwood? Even with Marshall away so frequently, it seemed improbable this could have happened without the family or the Talbots knowing.

Unless someone gained access to the house legitimately and stole the books then.

'Right, Kay, I have it.' Hector's serious tone snapped her out of her thoughts.

'If you could just turn to the inside of the back cover.'

She waited for a moment before continuing. 'Is there anything written in pencil in the bottom right-hand corner? It's probably very faint and could be difficult to make out.'

Hector's heavy sigh made Kay's heart sink. 'Yes, there's something here. Looks like a flower. No, it's three letters. Could be someone's initials. Barely visible but they're here all the same.'

'*THG*?'

Another pause and then, 'Yes, you're right. I can make them out clearly now.' Kay sensed Hector's realisation of what he had. 'I don't know, Kay,' he said. 'Sixty years in the business and this has never happened to me before.'

'I'm sorry,' Kay sympathised. 'It's come as a shock to me, too.'

'Who'd have thought it. From what I can recall the man seemed respectable enough. Well dressed. Not the type you'd reckon to be a criminal.'

'Can you describe him?'

'Average height, brownish hair. Pleasant enough face. Like I said, well dressed. Probably early twenties. Businesslike manner.'

Not much to go on, Kay considered. 'Mr Jackson would you mind withdrawing the book from sale?'

'Of course I'll withdraw it,' he was quick to agree. 'This is a matter for the police.'

'Naturally, but d'you mind if I have a word with the owner first before you contact them.'

'Whatever you want to do, Kay. I'll wait for you to get back to me.'

Her hand shaking slightly at the enormity of what she'd discovered, Kay replaced the receiver. How many more were out there? She still had a number of book dealers to call. But first she needed to contact Marshall. How, she frowned, would he take the news?

Mulling this over, she got up to see what Rachel had wanted just as her friend returned.

'You won't believe this,' she said, keeping her voice low. 'But after talking about Lucy's brother not approving of her boyfriend, he came in about five minutes ago asking to see you. I told him you were on the phone so he's been browsing the shelves while he waited.'

Kay frowned. 'Darren's back asking to see me?'

'No,' Rachel hissed. 'Marshall Garner. Thank goodness he didn't arrive earlier when they were here.'

Kay's heart turned over. 'I'll second that,' she breathed. 'His day's going to be difficult enough when I tell him what I've just learned.'

Rachel's eyes widened. 'What's happened?'

'One of the missing books has turned up. I'll tell you all about it later. I must give Marshall the news first.'

The moment she saw him standing in a quiet corner of the shop, his grim profile had her believing he'd seen Lucy and Darren after all.

She walked across to greet him. He turned and looked at her.

'Marshall, I've some news . . . ' Her voice tailed off.

His face was drained of colour.

'Whatever's wrong?'

'Jane Austen, *Sense And Sensibility*, first edition,' he said coldly.

She glanced at the small leather bound book he was holding.

'Part of your bequest and, correct me if I'm wrong, one of the so-called missing books.'

A chill ran down Kay's spine.

'How can it be?' She looked at him perplexed. 'Besides a book as valuable as that wouldn't be out on the shelves.'

'You don't believe me? Here, take a look. Oh and the final touch.' His eyes bore into her stricken face. 'Toby's special mark at the back. I'd say that just about confirms it. Wouldn't you?'

Kay took the book he thrust at her and looked at it in disbelief. 'But how . . . I don't understand?'

'And I can't believe it either. All

along you've taken me for a fool.
Tobias, too. Thank God he didn't live
to discover the truth.'

His words were like a physical blow.

'Marshall . . . I . . . you don't — '

He took her stumblings for guilt.

'Return the books not set aside for
you and no more will be said. I don't
want Lucy's faith in you shattered at
such a stressful time in her life, but it
goes without saying you will have
nothing more to do with her. How you
go about this, I'll leave to you. But
don't try my patience, Kay.'

11

Sleep did not come easy that night. Tossing and turning, Kay asked herself over again why Marshall had such little faith in her. How could he believe she would act so dishonestly?

Each time she asked the question the pain worsened. Again she relived the scene in the shop which ended with Marshall striding from the premises and leaving her with a sense of despair she'd never before experienced.

Rachel's initial disbelief that such a valuable book had somehow found its way on to the shop shelves, turned to the same bewilderment as Kay's.

Kay turned over again and curled up on her side. Dawn was breaking before restless sleep finally overcame her.

She woke late, disbelieving she had slept through her alarm. The radio clock was now reading eight-thirty.

She groaned as the enormity of the previous day's events crowded in on her. She sat up and got out of bed.

Friday, one of their busiest days of the week. Rachel would be here before she knew it.

A short time later, dressed in a tan skirt and a fine lavender sweater she made it down to the shop in a matter of minutes before Rachel arrived.

'How are you feeling?' Rachel greeted sympathetically, noticing the bruising shadows under Kay's eyes.

'Been better,' Kay sighed. 'I must ring Hector Jackson again.'

'I take it Marshall Garner doesn't know about the book Hector has?'

Kay gave her a wry look. 'I hardly got the chance to tell him.'

Rachel was all sympathy again. 'I wish I'd known what he'd accused you of before he left. He'd have taken it all back by the time I'd finished with him.'

Kay smiled. Rachel's loyalty meant a lot. 'Maybe it was just as well you didn't. Bookshops are supposed to be quiet, reflective places.'

Rachel raised a smile. 'You know what I mean. But you should tell him about the other book, Kay. Hector will back you up.'

'Oh, I don't know.' Kay's confidence remained at an all time low.

'You could always give him Marshall's number and ask him to repeat his story.'

Kay reflected for a moment. 'You're right. I'll try and get hold of him now.'

But each time she tried the bookshop's number, it was either engaged or the answer machine was on.

To try to overcome her frustration, she spent the next few hours dealing with customers and adding new stock to the shelves.

'I'll get that,' Rachel said as the phone began to ring. 'Yes, she's here,' she announced a moment later. She placed her hand over the mouthpiece. 'It's Hector Jackson. Say's it's urgent.'

Minutes later Kay replaced the receiver.

'What's happened now?' Rachel frowned.

'The man who sold the stolen book to him has just been back with the other two,' Kay explained. 'Hector made the excuse of not having enough cash on the premises to buy them. He guessed rightly he wouldn't accept a cheque so he told him he'd have to go to the bank. He's arranged for him to call back at four. That will give me enough time to drive over.' She checked her watch. 'I'd better go now.'

Rachel's eyes widened. 'On your own and without ringing the police first? Kay, it could be dangerous. You should get on to them before you do anything else.'

'But that could take ages. I haven't got time.'

'Then ring Marshall Garner. You can't do this on your own. It could turn nasty. You need someone like him with you.'

Kay saw sense. 'You think he'll believe me?' she said, reaching for the receiver and not holding out much hope.

Later Kay hurried out of the shop the minute Marshall pulled up outside.

The passenger door was opened for her the moment she crossed the pavement. She scrambled up and threw herself into the seat.

Marshall's expression was strained. 'Kay. Yesterday — '

'Not now,' she said stiffly. 'We haven't time. Let's get to Sheffield.'

Without another word, he put the vehicle into gear and pulled away. Some time later, with increasing frustration, Kay wished the road would clear as they inched their way through the heavy traffic approaching the city.

The journey had been a silent ordeal as Marshall concentrated on keeping to the speed limit.

'It's not far now,' she announced while he skilfully negotiated the traffic. He continued to follow her directions until the next turn took them closer to the quiet back street where Hector Jackson's shop was situated.

'Second right and we're there,' she

said a short time later.

Marshall shot her a glance. 'In that case, I'll park in the first. If this person is known to us, he could recognise the vehicle.'

Of course, Kay reflected. It was something she wouldn't have thought of if she'd been on her own.

As Marshall pulled into the kerb, she checked her watch and saw they had barely minutes to get to the shop.

Once out of the vehicle, she almost had to break into a run to keep pace with his long strides.

Her trepidation increased as they approached the book shop. Surprised that on such a chilly day, the front door was wide open, Kay stepped inside the shadowed interior with Marshall close behind to find the premises empty.

'Something's wrong,' she said, throwing him a worried look.

A muffled groan came from the rear of the shop.

'Sounds like someone's in trouble.' Marshall hurried over to the side of the counter. 'Over here, Kay.'

Her heart skipped a beat as he leaned down and she heard him say, 'It's all right, Mr Jackson. Can you get to your feet?'

As Hector confirmed he could and Marshall began to help him up, Kay was shocked to see how shaken the old man looked.

'Fiend pushed me over.' His breathing was laboured as he tried to explain.

'Let's get you to a chair,' Marshall encouraged. 'You can tell us all about it once you've got your breath back.'

Hector was soon made comfortable in the roomy armchair he'd used since Kay had come there as a child.

'Close the door, pet. And turn the closed sign round while I tell you what happened. You missed him by a matter of minutes.'

Kay's concern for the elderly bookseller overcame the disappointment this brought. 'Never mind about that, Mr Jackson. Now are you sure you're all right?'

'I'll survive. Just see to the door, please.'

While Marshall pulled up two stools from the side of the counter, Kay did the old man's bidding.

Once they were settled, Hector looked ruefully at them both. 'I'm afraid he got the better of me,' he began. 'Turned up sooner than I expected. I tried to stretch things out. Examined the books more than was necessary. In the end he must have sensed I was playing for time.'

'He still has them then.'

'Oh, yes,' Hector nodded to Marshall's question. 'Before I knew what was happening, he snatched the books up off the counter. I tried to make a grab for them but the next minute I felt the force of his hand on my chest and found myself on the floor.'

Inside Kay fumed that someone could act in such a brutal way towards a man she knew to be in his eighties.

'I think he arrived in a van,' Hector continued. 'One passed the window just before he came into the shop. Dark blue with something in red on the side. Heard an engine roaring seconds after he'd gone.'

'There's nothing like that parked outside now,' Marshall said. 'It must have been his.'

A blue van, Kay considered. Then alarm bells began to ring. She remembered the day Darren had collected the CDs. The van he'd been driving was blue. Her heart sank. He had access to Westwood and from what she could gather, almost always when Marshall was away?

And he'd been in her shop yesterday. How easy it would have been for him to slip the Jane Austen on to the shelf without anyone noticing. If this proved true, Lucy would be devastated.

'Well we have something to go on,' Marshall said. 'We can give a description to the police.'

'You can ring them from here now,' Hector said.

'Mr Jackson,' Kay interrupted, 'I've

got a theory about the thefts.' Aware of Marshall's frown, she asked, 'D'you mind if we wait a little longer before contacting the police?'

'Kay?' Marshall began.

'You have your suspicions,' Hector said at the same time.

She looked at them both and nodded.

'You mustn't put yourself at risk,' the old man warned. 'I've just experienced how violent that man can be.'

'I won't be reckless,' she assured him. She glanced at Marshall. 'And having Marshall with me — '

'You're right,' Hector broke in. He looked Marshall up and down. 'It would be a brave man to take you on.'

'I'm sorry, Mr Jackson,' Kay hastened. 'I've not introduced you. This is Marshall Garner, the owner of the stolen books.'

Marshall gave the old man a warm smile as he offered his hand. 'Pleased to meet you, Mr Jackson.'

'Would you give us another twenty-four hours?' Kay asked. 'If my suspicions come to nothing, I'll come back this time tomorrow and together we'll contact the police.'

She sensed Marshall was bursting with curiosity but he held back from asking what was on her mind.

'Do what you think best,' Hector decided. 'And now I'm going to call it a day.' He started to get up out of his chair.

'Are you sure there's nothing we can do,' Kay asked.

Hector shook his head. 'I'm fully recovered now. I'll lock up after you leave and look forward to hearing from you tomorrow.'

After saying goodbye, Kay and Marshall left the shop. Satisfied to hear Hector's son called to take his father home every day after work, they set off to where Marshall had parked.

'So, these suspicions?' Marshall asked the moment they were outside on the pavement, as she knew he would. She could tell from his tone he was beginning to lose patience. She shot him an anxious look. 'It's difficult,' she began. 'And hopefully I'll be proved wrong. But the van Hector mentioned.'

'Yes?'

'The van Darren was driving the other day when he dropped Lucy off — '

'Was blue,' Marshall finished.

Kay had never seen him looking so grim. 'That's right,' she said. 'I think where was something painted on the side, too.'

'If I thought for a minute,' she heard him mutter to himself. 'Come on.' He took her arm and increased their pace. 'It's time we did some more investigating.'

They had barely reached the main route out of the city when indications showed a traffic accident was causing gridlock.

'This is just what we need,' Marshall protested, slowing down to a crawl.

As their line of traffic inched further forward overtaking vehicles queuing on their right, the sight of a dark blue van just ahead made Kay's heart leap.

'Marshall, can you see,' she pointed. 'There's a blue van in the other lane.'

'Hardly likely to be the one we're after,' he rationalised. 'He'll be miles away by now. We couldn't be that lucky.'

'But we don't know how long the traffic's been held up.'

Kay knew she was clutching at straws but as they inched forward, closing the gap, her anticipation increased. A pattern of red chevrons painted against the blue, made her draw breath.

'There's a red design on the side,' she exclaimed excitedly.

Marshall shot her a glance. 'The same as Darren's?'

Kay hesitated. 'I don't know. I only caught a glimpse when he sped off.'

'We need to see who's driving,' Marshall said.

Anticipation that they might soon draw up alongside turned to disappointment. Just ahead, the traffic police had coned off part of the road and were now getting things moving again. Marshall's vehicle was brought to a halt while the other line of traffic was given priority.

Kay heard him curse under his breath when the van was lost to them.

Then it was their turn. Marshall skirted the scene of the accident and soon had them on their way.

'There's no other way off this approach to the motorway,' he encouraged, 'so if it is him, he's heading in the same direction as us.'

'Marshall, I think I can see him again,' she cried when a blue van accessed the motorway and shot over into the fast lane.

Within moments Marshall had done the same.

'There it is,' she breathed. The van was only a few vehicles ahead of them. The game of cat and mouse continued until Marshall said, 'I get the feeling he knows he's being followed.'

Kay glanced anxiously at the speedometer.

If the van driver increased his speed any more, she feared they would lose him. Then he indicated to come off at the next junction; the one they would take for home.

Her concern for Lucy increased. It was looking very much like it could be Darren after all.

Up ahead the traffic lights were turning amber.

'This could be our chance.' Marshall indicated to take the outside lane ready to pull up alongside but just as he drew near, the van shot off.

With the engine roaring the driver sped through the red light, leaving behind him the squealing of brakes and blaring horns of vehicles narrowly avoiding a collision.

12

With an air of despondency hanging heavily between them, Kay and Marshall arrived back at her flat.

Kay led the way into the kitchen and after dropping her bag on the table, pulled off her scarf and jacket and hung them both on the back of a chair.

'Tea?' she asked

'Please.' Marshall sat down at the table.

'It's so frustrating,' she sighed. 'We almost caught up with him.'

Marshall remained glum. 'It's looking very much like Darren's still in the picture.'

'But how can we go about proving it?'

'Right now, I've no idea,' Marshall confessed. 'This is going to take some thinking through.'

Leaving him to his thoughts, Kay

busied herself making the tea.

'Thanks,' he sighed when she placed a steaming mug in front of him. 'I'm more than ready for this.'

'Any ideas yet on where to start?'

Marshall sighed. 'Talk to Lucy, I suppose.'

Kay looked concerned. 'You'll have to be very careful.'

'Yes, I'm aware of that.'

'It's a pity the number plate was covered with dirt. It could have been checked.' Kay spoke her thoughts out loud.

'No doubt deliberate,' Marshall concluded. 'He'll probably keep it off the road now. Then when he thinks the time is right either get rid of it or have it re-sprayed. It looks like he could get away with it.'

Marshall finished his tea and pushed his chair back. 'No point in putting this off.'

Kay got up to see him out.

'I'll ring you after I've had a word with Lucy.'

He hesitated and she read fresh concern in his face. 'Yesterday . . . the Jane Austen.' He struggled for a moment. 'I think the shock of finding it in your shop robbed me of rational thought.'

Kay swallowed. The memory of it all still hurt so much. And yet, as he took hold of her shoulders and she felt the warmth of his hands penetrating the softness of her sweater, all she wanted to do was to fall into his arms.

She trembled slightly under his gaze.

'Can you ever find it in your heart to forgive me?'

'It hurt, Marshall,' she said in response, her eyes bright with unshed tears.

'Oh, my darling.' The next moment she was enclosed in the strength of his embrace.

He brushed the top of her head with his lips. 'If it was half the hurt I felt after I'd realised what I'd done, I'll spend a lifetime making it up to you. I promise.'

She raised her head. 'Just a lifetime,' she teased, knowing she would break down completely if she allowed the full meaning of his words to settle in her heart.

'And more,' he said quietly, his voice softening. 'I love you, Kay. I think I've been in love with you from the moment we met. But for some unfathomable reason I've been fighting it. Maybe I was afraid my love would not be returned.'

'You afraid?' She questioned softly. 'That seems an impossibility.'

'Not where your feelings for me are concerned.'

It was said with such quiet vehemence she knew she would never doubt him.

'Your love has been returned longer than you ever realised,' she smiled, capturing his grey eyes with her own.

With a groan his lips covered hers and she found herself swept up on such a tide of emotion she never wanted the feeling to end.

Eventually Marshall eased his hold of her. 'As much as I'm loathe to leave, I must get back and speak to Lucy.'

Marshall kissed her tenderly. 'I'll ring as soon as I can. Let you know how things have gone. The outcome will decide what we should do next.'

Once Marshall had left, Kay returned to the kitchen to make something for supper. Not feeling particularly hungry she decided on a salad. She had just begun to prepare it when the doorbell rang. Wondering who the caller might be, she checked the security spy-hole to see Niall waiting on the landing.

She frowned. Even though she'd agreed there were no hard feelings, things had changed between them. With some reluctance, she opened the door.

'You're totally within your rights to tell me to clear off,' he greeted her with a smile that would melt a heart of stone, 'but it's the first opportunity I've had to apologise for last Sunday.'

And with that he produced a bottle of red wine from behind his back.

'You're not busy . . . entertaining, anything like that?'

She shook her head. 'No, not at all. I was just preparing some salad.'

The twinkling of his blue eyes was a reminder of the times she'd enjoyed his company. His chatter, she decided, might stop her worrying about Marshall and Lucy.

Deciding his devil-may-care attitude would lift her mood she said, 'Feel like sharing?'

'Don't need asking twice,' he enthused, handing her the bottle.

Kay red the label and saw it was a top quality Pinot Grigio. 'Seems a little extravagant for what I have to offer,' she commented as she led the way into the kitchen.

'Turns a meal into a banquet,' Niall said.

Despite being in Niall's company, the evening dragged. Maybe it was the events of the day, Kay mused while Niall chatted on; his talk no distraction after all. She kept wondering how things were going at Westwood.

'And that's about it.' He picked up the bottle ready to fill her glass. 'Top up?'

Kay quickly put her hand over it. 'Not for me, thanks.'

'But you're still on your first,' Niall complained.

'Honestly, I'm fine,' she insisted.

Niall looked quite happy with her decision. 'Ah well, looks like I'll have to finish it.'

'D'you think that's wise?' From her calculations, Niall was already well over the limit for driving. 'I take it you came in your car?'

Niall shook his head. 'No. Didn't need it tonight. Left it at home.'

Kay relaxed again. For once he appeared to be acting in a responsible way.

He raised the bottle again. 'Sure?'

'Quite sure. It's been a particularly tiring day.'

'So how come today's been different from any other?'

In view of the relationship between Marshall and Niall, Kay decided not to go into detail. Instead she just shrugged. 'Oh, some days are busier than others.'

'And how's that cousin of mine?'

'He's fine. I've just finished the cataloguing,' she hedged.

Niall's eyes widened a little. 'Already? You'll be in the money now whether you sell yours or hang on to them for a while. Find the missing books?'

She shook her head. 'No, I didn't. Marshall said when he has time he might check the attics. There's always the possibility they could be up there. Now how about a coffee to finish off?' Without waiting for Niall's reply, she got up from the table.

Over at the sink unit, she reached up to pull down the kitchen blind. At the same time the security lights came on illuminating the car park.

For a moment Kay stood mesmerised, thinking her eyes were playing tricks. Over by the entrance, a familiar line of red chevrons stood out on the side of a parked van. She blinked and looked again. It was still there. But how . . .

She needed to phone Marshall. She turned quickly away from the window to find Niall standing right behind her.

'Looks like something's caught your eye. What is it?' he asked.

'There's a van parked outside,' she began.

Niall peered out over her shoulder. 'The one parked over there. It's one of the firm's. Comes in useful,' he grinned, 'no need for my car.'

'But it looks like the one we — ' she broke off. There was something behind Niall's smile; something cold and threatening.

'Followed back from Sheffield,' he finished.

Kay looked at him with utter disbelief. 'It was you?'

'Really, Kay. Did I make some kind of admission there? I don't think so.'

'But then how?'

'I could know the driver. There are other possibilities.'

She moved to slip past him. 'I need to call Marshall.'

His arm snaked out around her waist and he pulled her back against him.

'Please, Niall.' She struggled to free herself. 'Let me go.'

He spun her around to face him. 'Now why would I want to do that?' His breath, heavy with wine, fanned her face. 'Marshall can't have all the fun.'

Kay managed to twist around while Niall still maintained a firm grip on her arm. 'But he needs to know the van's here. You need to explain.'

Niall's laughter was chilling. 'I don't think so. What's more important is what I'm going to do with you, Kay. What a pity he got in the way. We would have made a great team.'

'With your expertise we could have siphoned the most valuable books from the collection. He'd never have known. Trouble for me, it's been a bit hit and miss.'

'So you are involved.' She felt sick inside. She remembered the Jane Austen. 'And you tried to incriminate me by leaving one of the books in the shop.'

'Ah, you found it.'

'Marshall did.'

'Even better.' Niall looked pleased with himself.

'It was easily done, although I had to resist the temptation of chatting up those pretty assistants of yours. Naturally I didn't want my presence noted. Hoped it would cause a bit of bother and shift Marshall's suspicions off me. Naughty, wasn't it?'

Niall's exaggerated pretence at being remorseful, confirmed Kay's fears that he was becoming more unstable by the minute.

'He's suspected I'd been wheedling money out the old man for years but Toby always stuck up for me. Thank goodness he got a bit confused this past year. Made things a lot easier.'

Seeing Niall for what he was, Kay's disgust increased.

'So,' he gave a theatrical sigh, 'like I said, just what am I going to do with you? Won't you come with me?' He cocked his head to one side. 'You won't, will you?'

'Never,' she retorted.

'Looks like I'll have to arrange a little accident then. Second time lucky,' he grinned. 'What d'you say?'

Kay's blood ran cold at the inference of what he'd just said.

'You'll only make things worse for yourself,' she tried desperately to rationalise the situation. 'Let me ring Marshall and ask him to come over. We could talk things through — '

'We stopped having civil conversations a long time ago,' Niall interrupted sharply, annoyance hardening his features.

And with that his grip on her arm tightened. 'What I need now is something to tie you up with while I think things through.'

He yanked her away from the window, pulling out one drawer after another until he found a ball of household string.

Kay began to panic and tried to lash out at him but he was too strong for her. Soon her wrists were tied together behind her back. She uttered a cry of fear as he flung her back on to the kitchen chair then fastened her bound hands to it.

The moment he's gone she would find a way to get to the phone.

'So, darling Kay,' Niall mused after taking his chair again at the table. 'I think the best thing would be to make it look like you've had too much to drink. And then, oh dear, under the influence you happen to cause a fire. Yes,' he slapped his hands on the table, 'that's it.'

'And how d'you propose to make me drunk,' Kay fought back while inside she had never been so frightened in her life. 'I'll never give you the chance.'

'Brave words,' Niall grinned. Then his expression changed again. 'Oh, Kay, this is such a waste. But it has to be done. Now where d'you keep your supply of booze.'

'There isn't any,' she said triumphantly. 'I only buy it in for special occasions.'

'And this isn't one of them?' Niall mocked. 'Never mind. I'll just nip across to the Weaver's and buy a few bottles. Trouble is I'm a bit strapped for cash. Now where's your handbag?'

Before Kay could respond the ringing of the doorbell was music to her ears.

Niall glared at her. 'You didn't tell me you were expecting someone.' He scrambled to his feet, snatched her scarf and used it to gag her before she'd had time to think about calling out. 'Now, if we just sit here quietly,' he said, 'they might go away.'

Kay prayed it was Marshall or even Rachel come to see how they had got on in Sheffield. Keith was bound to be with her.

But the ringing persisted until Niall finally lost patience. Snatching the empty wine bottle up off the table, he went into the hall closing the door behind him.

13

The moment Niall was gone, Kay struggled desperately to ease her hands free but it was hopeless. From the muffled sounds of voices, she knew he had answered the door.

If she stood any chance of being rescued she knew it was now or never. She struggled once more in the vain hope of releasing her hands, then inspiration struck.

With some effort she managed to push her chair back further away from the table. She raised her feet and positioned them under the edge of it.

Another push and her chair tilted back. For one frightening moment she thought it would continue to topple backwards until she'd crashed on to the floor.

Relief came when, with a thud, it stopped against the kitchen unit.

Using every last ounce of strength she forced the table up with her feet until it began to tilt.

The glasses were the first things to fall. Rolling down the sloping table, they disappeared over the edge to smash upon the tiled floor but Kay doubted the noise had been heard to any great effect outside the room.

She pushed again. The plates followed. Then one final push and the table toppled over. Exhausted but relieved, she imagined the noise would have been heard across the square.

Moments later the kitchen door flew open. Fear stopped her heart. Would she now have Niall's anger to face?

Relief was exquisite when Marshall's tall figure came staggering around it with one hand to his head.

'Kay?' His expression haggard, he took in the scene before him then stumbled through the debris to where she was sitting and untied the scarf.

Kay took a deep breath. 'That's better,' she gasped. 'The scissors are in the drawer behind me. Where's Niall?'

'Taken off,' Marshall said as he opened the drawer. 'Caught a glimpse of a wine bottle before he struck me on the head with it. It all happened so quickly. He'd been trying to make out you and he were having a cosy evening together. I was having none of it and was pushing my way in just as a crash sounded from the kitchen. Got them.'

Marshall took out the scissors and as he worked to cut her ties, Kay noticed a trickle of blood start down his forehead.

'Marshall, you're hurt.'

'It's nothing,' he dismissed. 'Niall didn't knock me out but it gave him the chance to get away. On two wheels I imagine,' he said dryly, 'judging by the screeching of the tyres.'

As the danger they'd both been in hit her, she flung her arms around him.

'Marshall,' she sobbed. 'He was going to set fire to the flat.'

She felt his body tense against her then he said softly, 'It's over, Kay. You're safe with me. Now let's get you into the sitting room away from all this mess.'

He helped her on to her feet and with his arm still around her, led her across the hallway into the sitting room where she insisted she staunch the flow of blood trickling down his face with a wad of tissues. Then for a long moment they held each other in silence.

Eventually Kay raised her head. 'I expect you've guessed Niall was behind the thefts,' she said, her voice troubled. 'And he was driving the van we followed. It belongs to the firm he works for.'

Marshall sighed. 'Despite suspecting Darren, I had misgivings about Niall. He was forever in debt. His drinking was getting out of hand and he could never hold down a job for long.' He looked at her for a long moment. 'Despite what he might have told you.'

'I was beginning to see the real Niall, Marshall,' she assured him. 'But what will you do now?'

'If it had just been the matter of the

books, I'd have dealt with it myself and not involved the police. Aunt Helen has suffered enough with his wild behaviour over the years.'

Kay noticed his jaw tighten. 'But after what you've just been through and what he did to Mr Jackson, well there's no question about it. They'll have to be told.'

Concern lined his face as he looked down at her. 'Is there anything I can get you before I call them?'

Kay gave him a loving smile. 'No, I'm fine. I just feel so tired.'

'In that case . . . ' He arranged some cushions at one end of the sofa and then tenderly helped her lie down against them. 'I want you to rest until they get here.'

It only seemed a moment from listening to Marshall begin to make the call until she felt the touch of his hand gently shaking her shoulder.

'Kay?'

She pulled herself up. 'Are they here?' she frowned.

He shook his head. 'Another ten minutes or so. There's — ' His voice broke.

She looked into his stricken eyes and felt a chill of fear. 'Marshall, what is it?'

He sat down beside her and took her hand. 'I began by saying there'd been an incident at your flat. The moment I gave the sergeant the details of Niall's van he put me on hold. I was wondering why when he came back on and told me they'd just had a report of a fatal accident. A vehicle had gone off one of the top roads and struck a stone barn. It matched the van's description. Apparently they'd just identified the driver by his licence.'

'Niall?' Kay whispered.

Marshall nodded.

'He'd drunk almost a bottle of wine.'

'Not unusual for him,' Marshall sighed. 'We'll know more when the police get here. I insisted I would break the news to his mother after we've given our statements. I told them there had been a family argument that had got a little out of hand. Hope you don't mind.'

'Of course I don't mind. No-one else need ever know what truly happened.'

Admiration filled his eyes as he said, 'I love you so much, Kay.'

'And I you,' she whispered.

She squeezed his hand. 'I think we'd better tidy up the kitchen before they arrive. If they see the state it's in they may ask more questions than we want them to.'

'And after I've broken the news to Helen, you're coming home with me,' Marshall insisted. 'With all you've been through, you're not spending the night alone.'

★ ★ ★

Kay woke early to the cheerful sound of birdsong. Then the previous night's events came crowding in on her and her heart became heavy with what they still had to face.

She remembered very little of the

journey back to Westwood; sleep having overcome her on the way there.

After Marshall's insistence they would talk in the morning, she had fallen thankfully into bed.

The statements they had given to the police were just a formality then Kay had remained at the flat while Marshall had visited his aunt.

She felt a rush of admiration for him then and now as she recalled his protection of his aunt, saying he would make the formal identification.

Remembering his promise to call into the station that morning, Kay turned her head quickly to check the time before scrambling out of bed.

She found Marshall outside on the terrace where Nesta had said he'd taken his coffee. She could see the burden of the previous night's events still hung heavily on his shoulders.

'Care for some company?' she said softly.

He got to his feet to greet her. 'Yes, please.'

She placed her cup down on the table alongside his and slipped into his arms.

'I'll drive you into town,' she offered as they sat down, worried he had spent a sleepless night.

In contrast to the beautiful spring morning, she could see sadness still shadowed Marshall's eyes.

He shook his head. 'I'll be fine.'

'Does Lucy — '

'Yes, I told her when she came down for breakfast.'

'How did she take the news?'

'She's upset, of course. In her eyes Niall could do no wrong.'

On Marshall's behalf Kay felt a huge sense of injustice. 'I think she should be told the truth.'

'Not yet, Kay,' he insisted softly. 'Maybe some time in the future and only if we feel it's necessary.'

She took his hand. 'You're right. It would serve no purpose other than being extremely upsetting for her.'

'So how are you feeling today?'

She sighed. 'Numb. I still can't

believe all that's happened.'

'I go cold each time I think of the consequences if I hadn't called round to your flat.'

Kay raised her face to him. 'That's what I've been meaning to ask you. What did bring you back?'

'It was all thanks to Lucy and I couldn't wait to tell you.'

'Lucy?'

'The talk I was going to have with her about Darren, remember? it wasn't necessary.' His features softened. 'Lucy had something to tell me instead. She came rushing into the hall the minute I walked into the house. I'm sure you'll be pleased to hear she and Darren are no more.'

Kay was amazed. 'I hope it was Lucy who ended the relationship.'

Looking pleased, Marshall nodded. 'She did . . . and how.'

'But why,' Kay frowned.

'The CDs he was forever borrowing off her. Seems he was making counterfeit copies and selling them at car boot sales and anywhere else he got the chance. One of his friends let it slip when she saw him in town. Been making quite a tidy sum, apparently.'

'That explains the gold chains and expensive watch,' Kay concluded, angry at the way Lucy had been used. 'Is she very upset?'

'Furious more than anything.' Marshall sighed. 'The tears came this morning when I broke the news about Niall's accident.'

'She must be devastated. Would you like me to have a word with her?'

Marshall nodded. 'I'm sure she'd welcome it.' He checked his watch. 'It's time I left. The sooner I get this over with the better.'

Kay glanced up at the house. 'I'll go up and see if Lucy wants a little company,' she suggested.

'Is it any wonder I love you,' Marshall said, drawing her into his arms.

Kay's heart filled with happiness. 'If only Tobias could see the outcome of his legacy,' she sighed. 'D'you think he'd be surprised?'

'I've been giving that a lot of thought,' Marshall said. 'And no, I don't think he'd be surprised at all.'

THE END

We do hope that you have enjoyed reading this large print book.

Did you know that all of our titles are available for purchase?

We publish a wide range of high quality large print books including:
Romances, Mysteries, Classics
General Fiction
Non Fiction and Westerns

Special interest titles available in large print are:
The Little Oxford Dictionary
Music Book, Song Book
Hymn Book, Service Book

Also available from us courtesy of Oxford University Press:
Young Readers' Dictionary
(large print edition)
Young Readers' Thesaurus
(large print edition)

For further information or a free brochure, please contact us at:
Ulverscroft Large Print Books Ltd.,
The Green, Bradgate Road, Anstey,
Leicester, LE7 7FU, England.
Tel: (00 44) **0116 236 4325**
Fax: (00 44) **0116 234 0205**

ALL TO LOSE

Joyce Johnson

Katie Loveday decides to abandon college to realise her dream of transforming the family home into a country house hotel and spa. With the financial backing of her beloved grandfather the business looks to be a runaway success. But after a tragic accident and the ensuing family squabbles Katie fears she may have to sell her hotel. When she also believes the man she has fallen in love with has designs on her business, the future looks bleak indeed . . .

ERRAND OF LOVE

A. C. Watkins

Jancy Talliman flies halfway around the world to Bungalan, in Australia, to renew an interrupted love affair with Michael Rickwood, who she'd met in London. She remains undaunted on discovering that he's unofficially engaged to Cynthia Meddow, especially given the support of Michael's brother Quentin, and his sister Susan. Jancy settles in a small town nearby. Then as she becomes involved with the townspeople, dam worker Arnulf, and Quentin, Jancy alters the very reason for her long journey south . . .

A NEW BEGINNING

Toni Anders

Rowena had only met her godmother once, so why had Leonora Lawton left Cherry Cottage to her in her will? Should Rowena sell her bequest and continue to run her successful children's nursery, or make a new beginning in the chocolate box cottage two hundred miles away? The antagonism of Kavan Reagan, her attractive neighbour, who had hoped to inherit the cottage himself, only strengthens her resolve to make a new life for herself.

DAYS LIKE THESE

Miranda Barnes

Meg is devastated when her husband, the unreliable Jamie, leaves her. But life goes on. She develops a friendship with a colleague, Robert. Then Meg makes the bittersweet discovery that she is pregnant with Jamie's child. When Jamie reappears, she can't bring herself to tell him he is to be a father — until it's too late . . . Baby James arrives, and Meg resolves to be as good a parent as she possibly can. But it's Robert, not Jamie, she misses . . .

LOVE AT FIRST SIGHT

Chrissie Loveday

How could anyone not fall in love with Cameron? Handsome, rich, funny, caring — the sort of man every girl dreams of. And he had fallen in love with Megan. She couldn't say 'no' to his offer of marriage and she was swept along in a whirl of preparations. Was he just too good to be true? How well did she really know him? What was the old saying — 'marry in haste, repent at leisure'? She just hoped the second part wasn't true . . .